FADING FROST

CRYSTAL FROST BOOK FOUR

ALICIA RADES

Published by Crystallite Publishing.

Produced in the United States of America.

Cover design by Clarissa Yeo.

ISBN: 978-0-9974862-4-7

To the members of my Facebook fan club. Thank you for supporting me throughout this whole series.

1

It's easier to accept death when you know there's an afterlife. I was certain of this fact because I'd seen ghosts and watched them cross over into the light before. Even so, I wasn't prepared to go.

As the car jerked to the right and I slammed on the brakes, all I could think was that I wasn't ready. Robin and I still had so much to experience together, and I knew Emma would be devastated if I was gone. What would happen when Mom's baby came? I would never get to know my little brother or sister. If I died right now, I wouldn't have even made a dent in my junior year of high school. No finishing up my first Varsity volleyball season. No junior prom. I'd die a virgin!

All of this went through my head in a split second. The car jolted when it passed over the edge of the road and into the ditch. I couldn't do anything to slow its momentum. Before I could process what was truly happening, the world tumbled around me, and my head smashed into something hard.

It took me several seconds to realize the car had come to a halt. A pain pounded through my head, and my vision blurred. I struggled to keep hold of my consciousness, like if I let my guard down for one moment, I'd fade. At least I was conscious enough to rejoice in the fact that I wasn't dead—even if the moment of joy lasted but a millisecond. I didn't know how long it took me to finally raise my head, but when I managed to blink the world back into focus, one thing was clear: for the first time in a long time, I had no idea what was going to happen next.

Shock overcame me, and I couldn't bring myself to cry even though I wanted to. I gulped down the terror rising to my throat, but that didn't slow my racing heart. When I finally managed to glance around the vehicle, I realized I had somehow lost control of the car, and when I hit the ditch, it had flipped. The side of my skull had connected with the driver's side window. I was lucky enough that the car had landed upright, and I didn't appear to have a broken bone or anything.

Slowly, I reached across the middle console toward my purse sprawled at the foot of the passenger seat. Something caught my body before my fingers touched the strap. I straightened up and tried again. This time, the seat belt stretched far enough so I could reach the purse and pull it onto my lap. I fumbled in search of my phone, ignoring the other contents that had flown from my purse just moments ago. The other line began ringing, and I put the phone to my ear.

"Hello?" my mom answered.

I pressed my free hand to my forehead, partially to ease the ache pulsing through my skull and partially to get myself to *think* about what to say to her. I must have remained silent for too long because my mother began speaking with a worried tone.

"Crystal, sweetie, are you okay?"

What could I say to that? Sure, my head was throbbing, but overall, I *was* physically fine. What about emotionally? I hardly had my license for two months, and already I was in an accident. As if that wasn't humiliating enough, my sixth sense immediately felt hazy. Although I'd only known about my psychic abilities for a year, I suddenly didn't feel like myself anymore.

"I'm okay," I half-lied, forcing down the bile in my throat. The truth was, I was riled enough to puke the entire contents of my dinner onto Teddy's steering wheel. I decided to focus on my physical state so I wouldn't worry my mother. Who knew what stress would do to my little brother or sister?

"But something's wrong," she concluded based on my minimal words and croaky voice.

I pressed my hand harder against my face like that would ease my headache and help me figure out what to say to her. I remembered the time Robin had called Teddy and told him about the car when a stranger slashed our tires. I decided to ease into it slowly by taking his approach.

I forced a painfully fake laugh. "Um . . . What if I told you something bad happened to the car?"

"Oh, my gosh, Crystal. What happened? Are you hurt?" At least she was less concerned about the damage I'd done to the car and more concerned about me.

"I'm not. It's just a headache." I lightly grazed my fingers across the goose egg-sized lump I already felt forming along my hairline. It immediately stung. I pulled my fingers away from the injury and saw they were covered in a layer of blood. The blow against the window must have split my skin open. "And a minor scratch," I added, though I wasn't sure how honest those words were. Truth be told, it hurt like *hell*. I quickly glanced into the rearview mirror and noticed it looked as bad as it felt. I was pretty sure I'd be alright, but that didn't stop a wave of hysteria from overcoming me.

"Tell me what happened," my mother insisted. "Were you speeding?"

I couldn't stop the words from tumbling out of my mouth. "What? No. Mom, I'm a good driver. I swear. It's just—I don't know. I lost control somehow. One second I was on the road, and then the next—"

"Crystal," my mother stopped me before I could hyperventilate. "It's going to be okay. We'll call an ambulance." I heard a shuffling in the background and my mother's muffled voice as she spoke to Teddy.

"No, Mom," I tried to tell her, but she didn't hear me. The phone shook in my hand.

A second later, she was talking into the phone again. "I'm going to keep you on the line while we call an ambulance with Teddy's phone, okay? Where are you? How long ago did you leave Robin's?"

"Mom," I stated sternly so she'd listen to me. "I'm only five minutes from Peyton Springs. It will be faster if you or Teddy come and get me." Our town was so small that our ambulance service came from the next town over.

"That doesn't change the fact that I'm still calling an ambulance. We'll be there soon. Stay put."

Where else would I go? the snarky 16-year-old in me wondered, but I kept quiet.

Mom kept me talking as she and Teddy rushed out to meet me on the secluded highway. I pressed some tissues to my gash as I waited, but it stung and didn't seem to help the bleeding. During a brief silence when my mom turned her attention to Teddy, I couldn't hold it in any longer. The pain in my head and the fright I'd felt when it happened all caught up to me. Tears sprang to my eyes and rolled down my cheeks.

My mom's vehicle was the first I saw after the car had flipped. When I spotted it, I finally hung up the phone. I hadn't moved and was still buckled in my seat.

"Crystal!" my mother exclaimed when she exited

the car. She rushed across the road to the vehicle I sat in and pulled on the door, only it didn't budge. "It's locked, sweetie." She gestured to the lock on the door.

Still slightly dazed, I unlocked the door. She opened it, but my step-dad was the one who knelt next to me, cupping my face in his hands.

"Are you okay?" he asked calmly. I didn't know how he remained so calm; it probably had to do with his police training.

Tears welled in my eyes again, and all I could do was nod.

Teddy reached up to take the tissues from my hand. "Here, let me help with that." He pulled the wad away from my face to inspect the wound before dabbing it against my forehead again.

I winced.

"That's a nasty gash," he said, stating the obvious.

I sniffled. "Can we go home?"

Teddy shook his head as a look of apology settled over his face. "We need to get you to the hospital first. You could have a concussion."

"No, I want to go home," I argued, but my voice came out sounding like a whisper.

"You're going to the hospital. Andrea?" he addressed my mother.

"He's right, sweetie," she agreed.

My gaze flickered between each of their eyes. "Okay," I agreed, but only because I loved them so much, not because I thought I actually needed to go.

We'd settled that argument, but nobody moved for several minutes as we waited for emergency responders to arrive. The chilly night air rushed in through the open driver's side door and filled the car.

Teddy finally stood and let my mom kneel beside me. He rested his hands on his hips and eyed the car. It was crumpled on all sides, though I was grateful there weren't any trees nearby that could have signed my death warrant. I was lucky enough to miss the telephone poles lining the road, too. He rounded the car to assess the damage before he spoke. "Looks like you blew a tire. I can't think of why, though. These tires aren't that old."

I pondered his statement for a moment, and that's when I realized it was all my fault. "Uh, I blew that tire up at a gas station before leaving the city. Robin said it looked low."

Teddy gazed at me. "Did you check the pressure?"

I shook my head guiltily. I didn't know anything about cars. I didn't even know if Teddy had a pressure gage in the car or, if he did, where to find it.

"It's okay," he finally said. "I'm just glad you're alright." Just then, his eyes locked on something in the distance, and that's when I noticed the emergency responders approaching in the rearview mirror. "I'll stay here while you two go to the hospital," he offered.

We all agreed that was a good idea. The rest of the night was a blur, but I remembered they let Mom ride with me in the ambulance.

"Don't fall asleep," she demanded when I lolled

my head to the side. "You could have a concussion."

"I'm not sleeping," I told her truthfully.

"You need to keep talking so we know you're okay." She exchanged a glance with the EMT as if to ask whether she was right or not.

"I'm okay, Mom," I insisted. "I just need to collect my thoughts."

She seemed to accept this and gave me several minutes to digest what had happened. When she noticed I was crying, she attempted to comfort me.

"It's okay, sweetie. I know Teddy loved his car, but we're just glad you're okay."

Little did she know, I wasn't crying about the damage I'd done to the car. The real reason I was crying was for a pain that was practically eating me whole. Something I couldn't quite pinpoint felt *off* about my abilities, and that terrified me to the depths of my soul.

2

The doctors gave me stitches and bandaged my wound. They said there was a good chance I had a mild concussion, but there wasn't really anything they could do but send me home with instructions to get plenty of rest.

"You don't have to go to school tomorrow if you don't want to," my mom offered on the way home after Teddy had picked us up with her car.

"I'm fine," I told her half-honestly. "I don't want to miss volleyball practice."

"Are you sure that's a good idea?" She eyed me from the passenger seat.

"It will be fine. If I miss it, I'll have to make it up. But if I feel dizzy or anything, Coach Kathy should let me sit out, or I can help Derek and be co-manager for the day."

She looked to Teddy in the driver's seat as if he might be able to reason with me. When he didn't say anything, she turned back toward me. "Do you still want to take that campus tour on Wednesday?"

"Mom," I practically snapped, "you're worrying too much. I'll be fine. Besides, I promised Kelli and Justine I'd be there. We were going to meet up and have lunch."

The campus tour Mom mentioned was a field trip to Southern Minnesota University for all interested seniors. The only problem was that they didn't have enough people interested, and they needed two more to get approval to take the bus. Our guidance counselor, Mrs. Blake, suggested Emma and I come along even though we were only juniors. Mrs. Blake knew my mom attended SMU and thought I might be interested, and she was right. Although I didn't know what I wanted to do for a career, I wanted to go to college, and it made sense to go there. It was only an hour away, so I could visit my family often. It was actually a closer drive to Robin's college than my current drive was, too. Plus, a lot of the kids from our school went there, so I would know some people, especially if Emma decided to enroll at SMU. We could even be roommates.

"Mom," I wondered aloud, "why did you choose SMU?"

She glanced back at me. "What do you mean?"

"I'm just thinking about how Mrs. Blake asked me

to go on the tour. She thought I might want to attend SMU because you did. I haven't really thought about my options and was just curious if SMU is the right choice for me. And I'm interested in why you didn't choose a college closer to your home so you could visit your family."

My mom let out a puff of air that sounded like a laugh. "Crystal, I know you and I get along, but your Grandma Ellen wasn't the easiest person to get along with at the time. Besides, I was young and interested in getting out on my own. I chose SMU because they had a good psychology program."

"Why'd you choose psychology? You don't even use your degree."

She pressed her lips together. "I wanted to do more with my degree at the time. I thought majoring in psychology would help me understand my abilities better and that maybe I could use them to help people — as a counselor or something. But then I met Sophie and Diane, and my ideas about my future changed. Diane was majoring in business, and so we came up with the idea of Divination together. We moved to Peyton Springs because it's where Sophie grew up, and there's a long line of psychics in the area. They help keep our business running even though everyone else just thinks we sell magic sets, Halloween costumes, and chocolate. Starting a business with my best friends was one of the best decisions I've ever made."

"So, do you think SMU is right for me?"

She shrugged. "I can't say I would be against you going there. I'd like you to be able to visit every now and then, but I don't want you to feel pressured if there's somewhere else you'd like to go."

I didn't even know what I would major in, but it was encouraging to know my mom had a good college experience there. "I guess we'll see how I feel about it on Wednesday," I finally said as we pulled into the driveway.

***

I fell onto my bed and shoved my face into my pillow. I immediately recoiled when a pain shot through my head. Not the smartest idea, although it didn't hurt as badly now as when the accident happened. I rolled over to my back and pulled the covers over my body. Before I had a moment to even *think* about crying, my mom knocked on my door and opened it a crack.

"Crystal, do you need anything before bed?"

I was about to tell her she was fussing too much, but I appreciated the sentiment. "No, Mom. I'll be fine. Thanks for asking." I could have told her about what was really going on—that my sixth sense felt off—but I didn't want to worry her, not with a baby on the way.

"Hey, Mom," I called before she shut the door completely.

"Yeah?" She opened it again, casting a strip of light from the hallway onto my bed.

"How's the baby?"

We'd only discovered in August that Mom was pregnant, though she and Teddy had been trying since their wedding last spring. Honestly, they were surprised to have gotten pregnant so quickly since they were both in their late 30s. They wouldn't be able to learn the sex of the baby for another few weeks, but Mom and Teddy decided they didn't want to know anything unless something was wrong. They wanted to be surprised when it came.

My mother's silhouette shifted in the doorway. "Why do you ask?"

I went silent for a few seconds before answering. "I just—I know tonight was really stressful, and I don't want the stress to affect the baby or anything."

She pushed into the room and sat on the edge of my bed. She rested a hand on her belly, which was still pretty flat. I shifted and placed my hand next to hers, even though there wasn't actually anything to feel.

"There's no reason to worry," my mother assured me.

I tore my gaze from her belly and looked up at her. "It's just . . ." I paused and then swallowed. "I already love her." I had bet on it being a girl, but my mom thought it'd be a boy. "Or him," I added, pressing my ear to her belly.

She jumped slightly in surprise before relaxing.

"I really love her—him," I said against her belly before pulling away. "You just worry about my little brother or sister. I'll be fine."

She smiled at that and then kissed my forehead. I took it as an agreement, but then she twisted her mouth in amusement and said, "Fat chance of that. I'm your mom. It's my job to worry about you."

"It's just a *scratch*," I lied. Luckily, the room was fairly shadowed so she couldn't see the worry written all over my face.

"I know." She smoothed down my hair. "But right now, it sounds like you're more worried about me being worried than I am worried about you."

I started to nod and then replayed what she'd just said in my mind. "Wait . . . what? That was confusing."

"Don't worry about it," she teased with a smile.

"You just worry about growing me a healthy brother or sister," I told her before kissing her belly and telling her goodnight.

"I love you, Crystal," she said before shutting my bedroom door and leaving me in darkness.

While my mother's company helped take my mind off the accident, I couldn't help it when I replayed it in my head as soon as she left. I pulled my stuffed owl Luna down from her shelf like I did every night and snuggled her close to me. Tonight, I needed the extra comfort.

I wasn't even that upset about the accident itself. If everything had happened like it did but I still felt my abilities inside me—if I felt like myself—I'd be fine. But the fact was that something was *wrong*. I couldn't explain it. I couldn't put it into words, but I knew it was happening to me nonetheless.

I should have called my boyfriend, Robin, or my best friend, Emma, right away. I knew one of them would make me feel better, but somehow, I felt like I couldn't explain *this*. So instead, I called out to the darkness.

"Daddy?" I said in a whisper. I clung to the stuffed animal he'd given me as a gift before he died. I had no way of knowing if he could hear me from the other side. Even when I had my gift, I'd never made contact with my father or felt him there with me. Still, I'd been talking to him — in a way — for the last few months whenever I felt I couldn't talk to a living person.

I fell asleep after asking my father for protection.

3

"Feel free to take notes and pictures once we reach campus," Mrs. Blake announced as we neared SMU on Wednesday.

Emma sat next to me on the bus, and I twisted my hands nervously in my lap. I had been excited about visiting SMU earlier this week, but the closer we got, the more anxious I became. It was like the idea of growing up had finally hit me, and I wasn't ready to think about college yet.

"You'll have the chance to talk to our tour guides as well as other students about their experiences," Mrs. Blake continued. "Take advantage of these opportunities, but don't forget that for most of you, this is your first campus tour. The school will host a couple more field trips throughout the year; however, most of you will also attend other tours with your parents."

"Crystal," Emma said in a low voice while Mrs. Blake continued talking toward the front of the bus. "What's up?"

My eyes flew to hers. "What do you mean?"

"You're practically strangling your sweatshirt," she pointed out, gesturing down to the sleeve I'd been twisting around in my hand. "You've been acting weird all week, ever since your car accident."

I relaxed my grip on my shirt and swallowed. I still hadn't told Emma — or anyone, for that matter — about what really happened to me, about how after I hit my head, my sixth sense had gone hazy. I hadn't been able to predict the lunch menu all week, something I'd once had a 100 percent success rate with. Every time I subtly tested my skills over the last three days, I hadn't been able to feel anyone else's emotions through touch. On one level, it left me feeling empty and alone. I'd become so used to being in tune with the people around me that it was strange to go back to normal — the way I'd been before puberty hit and my abilities manifested. On another level, I felt frightened, as if I would never get my abilities back. I wasn't quite sure why I hadn't mentioned it to anyone. Maybe I didn't want to admit it, like that would make the situation more real. A year ago, I may have rejoiced in this news, but now it only left me worried.

Luckily, Emma and I had been so busy with volleyball, homework, and boyfriends that our psychic practice sessions had slowed down. So far this week, I hadn't had to show my weakness in front of her. I knew she'd find out sooner or later, but I was hoping I'd feel better at the "later" point and my abilities would be back to normal.

Robin had freaked out when I told him about the accident. I could only imagine how scared he was to hear I'd crashed. He'd been in a bad accident a few years ago and lost his left leg from the knee down. I assured him on the phone I was okay. That seemed to calm him down, but even after a few days, I hadn't called him back to tell him about my gift fading.

"It's not the accident," I lied to Emma. I glanced her way quickly before fixing my eyes back on my hands. She didn't seem to notice my dishonesty, which was a victory for me. "I've just been nervous about this campus tour." Okay, that wasn't a complete lie.

"I know. Me, too," she agreed.

I let out an inaudible sigh of relief.

"I was excited at first," she continued. "I mean, we're only juniors, and already we're being all responsible and thinking about college, but now it's kind of scary. I mean, it's *college*. I have no idea what to expect."

"Yeah," I agreed. In all honesty, I added, "Me, either." The resounding truth of that statement sent a shiver down my spine.

***

Kelli and Justine waved to us from across the dining hall. Our field trip group was halfway through our tour, and we each received a meal voucher at the campus's buffet. Emma and I made our way over to them after we filled our plates.

"Hi," I greeted cheerfully.

They both stood, and we all exchanged hugs. After I'd helped rescue Kelli from an abusive relationship a year ago — with Justine's help — we'd become friends. Thanks to my abilities, I saw their friend Olivia's ghost, who held the key to saving Kelli. When they graduated, Kelli and Justine both headed off to college at SMU. I sat, wondering if more of our classmates would join us since they all knew Kelli and Justine, too, but no one did.

"What happened to you, Crystal?" Kelli gestured to the stitches on my head.

My hand came up to graze them lightly. "I, uh, had an accident."

"She blew a tire and flipped her car," Emma clarified.

"Oh, I'm sorry," Kelli told me.

"No, it's okay. My head hit the window, and that split the skin open. It's okay, really."

"Well, it kind of sucks," Justine said slowly.

I nodded. "So, how's your freshman year going?" I remembered Mrs. Blake's instructions to ask students about their experiences.

"It's great," Kelli beamed. Her voice was so full of happiness, completely opposite of the Kelli Taylor I'd known just a year ago. And then there was her new look. She'd dyed her hair a dark blond—closer to her natural color—and a small diamond stud now adorned her nose. It suited her well.

"It's okay," Justine shrugged.

"Just okay?" Emma asked skeptically. "That's not encouraging."

Justine laughed. "No, it's great, but . . ."

"But what?" I prodded curiously.

Justine glanced around the room. "Honestly? The campus gives me the heebie jeebies."

Kelli burst into a fit of laughter, and Justine joined in. I suspected there was some sort of inside joke I was missing.

"What do you mean?" Emma asked.

"Oh, it's nothing, really," Justine assured us.

Kelli laughed again. "Justine has a stalker."

I tensed for a moment. "A stalker?"

"No, I don't," Justine defended, swatting lightly at Kelli.

"She says she feels like she's being watched," Kelli teased. "I think it's that kid who sits behind us in psych. He's a creep."

My nerves subsided when I realized Justine wasn't in any real danger from a stalker. It really was just an inside joke I was missing out on.

"So," I said once I swallowed my potatoes, "Mrs. Blake says we're supposed to ask students about their experience at SMU. Why'd you guys choose this school?"

Justine gave a light eye roll. "Ha! Mrs. Blake. She's great but so serious. I remember doing campus tours with her. It's so different in college."

"How many colleges did you tour before choosing SMU?" Emma asked.

"Honestly," Justine said, "not many. I always knew I was going to go to SMU. It's close to home, and the tuition is decent. My mom and my aunt — you know, my aunt Sophie — both went here, so I've known my whole life that I'd end up here, too."

I nodded. It made sense. "And you, Kelli?" I asked before biting into more potatoes.

She shrugged. "Same reason, I guess — location and tuition. And I got lucky that my best friend came with me. We get to be roommates for the next four years!"

I glanced over at Emma, and she was eyeing me with a smile. I didn't have to be psychic to read my best friend's mind, which was saying, *We could be roommates here, too!*

"So, do you think you two will apply here your senior year?" Justine asked.

Emma nodded enthusiastically. She'd been in a state of pure glory all day during the tour.

"Yeah, maybe," I answered. "I think it's either going to be this or where Robin goes."

"That's right," Kelli said. "What's your boyfriend doing now? Still playing music?"

"Not as much as he did in high school. He's

majoring in occupational therapy."

"And your boyfriend, Emma?" Justine asked. "You two are still dating?"

Emma straightened in her chair. "Me and Derek? We've never been better! He bought me flowers and took me to a concert for my birthday last month. It was so sweet!"

"Aww," Kelli and Justine sang together.

"You two are cute together," Justine said. "I always saw you watching him at volleyball practice last year when he was catching balls. I'm surprised it took you two so long to get together."

Emma smiled. "Yeah, well, it was worth it."

I didn't say anything as they talked about the cute boys in their classes and student organizations. Eventually, their conversation faded into the background until it felt like I was secluded in my own little bubble and the rest of the cafeteria ceased to exist. My sixth sense tingled, a sensation that spread through to my fingertips. Joy overcame me when I realized what this meant. My abilities hadn't been destroyed in the accident!

I glanced around the dining hall, searching for the source of my feeling. It was only when I scanned the room for a second time that I noticed him. My eyes locked on a dark figure standing across the cafeteria, causing the sensation in my body to intensify. I knew immediately that no one else could see him because I was the only person I knew who could see ghosts.

Something about him was different, though. I couldn't make full features of him. Instead of looking like the other people milling about the hall, he appeared as just a shadow, dark with a hazy outline. Even though I couldn't see definite eyes, I knew he was looking my way.

***

I remained quiet on the bus ride back to the high school, the whole time contemplating what it meant to see a ghost but not being able to see what he really looked like. After thinking about it for some time, I came to the conclusion that he appeared fuzzy because my accident caused my abilities to work inefficiently. At the very least, seeing a ghost on campus meant my abilities weren't completely lost to me. I might actually be able to keep this minor hiccup a secret before I had to admit my newfound weakness to anyone.

But why had I seen a ghost in the first place? Did he need my help? How could I help him when my abilities weren't working well?

I decided I'd try a few psychic exercises at home after volleyball practice in hopes of connecting with the ghost. Then Emma's voice pulled me from my thoughts.

"So, what do you think? Still want to go to SMU?" Her tone was full of excitement.

What could I say to that? If I said I still wasn't sure, it would break her heart, but if I told her I wanted to go there and decided against it later, that'd be even more heart breaking.

"Well, we both still have a lot of schools to look at. Are *you* sure you want to go to SMU?"

The question was silly. Emma had purchased a butt load of SMU-branded goods from their campus store while we were there—a hoodie, a t-shirt, even a notebook. Though she said she was nervous about the campus tour, I could tell that if she had the choice, she'd graduate early and start classes next semester. She'd already pegged SMU as her school. I'm not sure why, maybe because she already had it figured in her mind that I was going to go there and she didn't want to leave her life-long best friend.

Emma nodded enthusiastically in response to my question.

"Do you even know what you'll major in?" I asked.

Her face fell. "I don't, but I have a lot of time to figure it out. Maybe music? Do you have any idea what you'd major in?"

I took a deep breath. I didn't know. I didn't have the slightest clue. For the last year, I'd wanted to do something with my abilities—maybe go into the police force or something, in which case I wouldn't have to go to SMU, which is why I wasn't ready to make that decision. *Now that it looks like my abilities might be failing me, maybe I should study something else*, I thought.

I averted my gaze from Emma's watchful eye and began to scan the rest of the bus in search of some sort of answer to give her. I was spared the hassle of answering when I looked to my right and came face-to-face with a black shadowy figure. His face didn't have any features, but it was hovering just inches from my own.

My heart leapt in fright, and I screamed.

4

Even if my abilities were in peak condition, I couldn't have anticipated what happened next. My scream of terror hardly had a chance to fill the bus before I felt my body lurch and I went flying across the center aisle. If the shadowy ghost was still there, I would have fallen straight through him. I flung my hands out to catch myself against the seat across the aisle. I managed to prevent myself from sliding into a senior named Jackie Smith, but I couldn't keep my right knee from smashing into the seat's metal frame. Emma's weight slid into me, and Jackie's head smacked against the window. An intense pain throbbed in my knee.

A moment later, the initial shock had subsided and everyone was rubbing at their aches and pains. A few people stood to piece together what had just happened.

I couldn't manage to move for a few seconds. All I could do was remain frozen with my hands on Jackie's seat and my body situated in the center of the aisle.

Did I cause that with my scream? I wondered.

Then, the bus broke out in a buzz of voices.

"What was that?"

"What happened?"

"Is everyone okay?"

"Crystal," Emma said, resting a hand on my back and leaning in to view my face. "Are you okay?"

I finally shifted to look at her. "I—I'm not hurt." It wasn't actually an answer to her question, and it was a complete lie because my knee was burning in pain. For a second, I was scared that I actually shattered my knee cap, but when I shifted to sit back next to Emma in our seat, I knew it wasn't that bad. "I just hit my knee. Are you okay?"

Emma nodded. She didn't appear to have hurt anything.

"Jackie?" I asked, looking over at her.

She nodded, too, although she was rubbing her head. "I'm fine."

Once I was sure everyone around me was okay, I finally looked toward the front of the bus to see if I could understand what had just happened. Gazing out the windows, I could see that the bus had swerved and now sat unmoving across both lanes of traffic. Although we had been driving along a rural highway, one car coming from the opposite way had already stopped, and another was slowing down behind it. Between the bus and the first car, I saw what had really happened.

My scream hadn't caused the bus to swerve. A huge tree lay crossways in the road just in front of us. It had pulled the power lines down around it. The top of the dead tree lay sprawled in the field to our left while the rotten stump appeared mangled to our right.

"Is everyone okay?" Mrs. Blake repeated.

By now, everyone appeared to be back in their seats, although some were standing and assessing the damage to the power lines. Our bus driver turned around in her seat and brushed the hair out of her face. Mrs. Blake was already beginning her way down the aisle to make sure everyone was okay. Then our bus driver, Mrs. Peterson, spoke up.

"Who was the one who screamed?" she asked sternly.

My heart dropped in my chest. Could I really be blamed for this? I mean, it's not like I had super powers where I could tip a tree with my voice. I bit my lip and looked at Emma nervously.

"Who screamed?" she asked again just as Mrs. Blake passed by our seat and headed further to the back of the bus.

I raised my hand nervously. "It—it was me." My voice came out so quiet that it sounded like a whisper.

"Crystal Frost, right?" she asked, making her way toward me.

I nodded sheepishly.

Then Mrs. Peterson stuck her hand out. I eyed it. What was I supposed to do with her hand?

"Thank you," she said, completely taking me off guard.

Oh. She wanted me to shake it. But why?

"If you hadn't seen the tree tipping and screamed, I wouldn't have noticed."

My mouth hung open. I shyly took her hand, not daring to admit that wasn't the reason I had screamed.

***

The rest of the day passed by in a haze. We sat around for a while to make sure everyone was okay and that the school knew what was going on. I called my mom's cell, but she didn't answer since she was at work. I left a message assuring her I was alright.

Our miracle of a bus driver managed to turn the bus around and get us headed back to the school on an alternate route. School had already let out by the time we got back.

"Ready for volleyball practice?" Emma asked with little confidence when we stepped off the bus.

"I don't think I'll be ready for practice until next season," I said half seriously.

Emma and I hurried to the locker room. Luckily, there were still a few girls getting into their practice gear, which meant we weren't late. Already this week, Coach Kathy had made me take it easy because she didn't want my head wound getting ripped open by a flying ball. I was grateful for that because I didn't want to have to dive for the ball with a bruised knee, even if I was wearing knee pads.

Once all the girls cleared out of the locker room, Emma spoke. "Are you going to be okay?"

I pulled on my shoe and began tying it. "What? Me?"

"Yes, you." She swatted at me with the t-shirt she was holding before pulling it over her head. "Is there anyone else here?" She looked around nervously when she realized what she'd just said. "Wait, there isn't, is there?"

I looked up to meet her gaze, but she was still scanning the locker room like she expected a ghost to reveal itself from behind the lockers.

"No, there's not, but—" I stopped mid-sentence. I hadn't wanted to tell anyone about losing my abilities for the better part of the week, so should I even bother telling her about the shadowy ghost I saw?

"But what?" Emma eyed me suspiciously. "Oh," she said slowly, realization dawning. "I was wondering how you saw the tree falling from where we were sitting. That's not why you screamed, was it?"

Boy, she caught on quickly. I shook my head.

"Who was it? What did they say?"

I shook my head again. "I have no idea, and he didn't say anything. I saw him on campus first, and then when I saw him on the bus, it kind of scared me." I didn't have to tell her he looked hazy and like a shadow, did I?

"'Kind of?' Crystal, that was the scream of 'bloody murder.' You don't know what this ghost wants?"

I shook my head for a third time and pressed my lips together. "I have no idea."

"Well," Emma said while tying her shoe, "you'll figure it out, like always. Let's get out there before Coach Kathy makes us run extra laps."

I quickly double knotted my second shoe and jumped up from the locker room bench to follow her into the gym. I split off in a different direction and found my way to Coach Kathy. All the other players were just getting started with stretches. "Coach?" I asked.

She looked at me expectantly.

"I, uh, don't know if you heard, but some of us on the field trip today were in a minor accident. I hit my knee," I peeled back my knee pad to show her the bruise that was forming, "and I was just wondering if I could help Derek again."

Coach nodded. "That's fine, Crystal. I don't want you getting into it too much until you get your stitches out next week anyway. Just don't cross the court when we're practicing serves. I don't want any balls hitting your stiches."

I nodded and then joined my team for stretches — at least those were safe enough. As soon as balls began flying, I headed over to Derek. Derek was one of my best friends and Emma's boyfriend. He was also our team manager, which meant he helped keep track of stats during the games and helped run drills during practice.

"Hey, Derek," I greeted. "I guess it's back to co-manager duties for me again today."

"Sounds good." He smiled. "Hey, I heard what happened to you guys after the campus tour. Are you both alright?"

"I hit my knee, but we're fine."

"I haven't had a chance to talk to Emma. She's okay? You're sure?"

It was cute how he seemed so worried about her. I knew Robin would act the same way, like he did when I'd told him about my first accident, but I still had to tell him about what happened today on the bus. "Derek, she's fine."

"Okay. Thanks for letting me know. I'll catch the balls along the edge of the court if you get the ones that go across the gym. I'd hate to see your stitches get ripped open."

"But if they did, maybe I could keep them until Halloween," I joked. "I'd make a great Frankenstein— or maybe a zombie."

Derek let out a laugh before heading to throw some balls back onto the court for the girls who were practicing their serves.

Last year, Emma, Derek, and I had dressed up in a trio costume for the Peyton Springs Halloween Festival. Derek was the Cat in the Hat and Emma and I were Thing 1 and Thing 2. Now the festival was just a few weeks away again, and I still didn't know what I was going to be. I could drag out my costume again from last year, but Emma had already talked about doing a couple's thing with Derek. Maybe Robin and I could do something together. If I was smart, I'd go as the same thing every year like my mom did so I wouldn't have to worry about choosing a new costume every Halloween. She always went as a gypsy and hosted a tarot card reading booth—and no one had figured out yet that it was the real deal!

I threw a couple of balls at my teammates as they practiced their spikes but sat out when they played a scrimmage at the end of practice.

Normally, I would walk home with Emma, but she headed in the opposite direction with Derek after practice to work on homework for their government class—a class I wasn't taking this semester. At least, that was her excuse. In reality, "homework" was probably code for "making out," but I didn't say anything.

I walked home from practice alone, the hairs on the back of my neck standing straight up the entire way.

5

"I'm fine," I assured Robin when I called him that evening. For some reason, I couldn't bring myself to tell him I saw a ghost on the bus. I told Emma—even if I didn't tell her the whole truth—but I felt if I mentioned any of it to Robin, he would worry too much. His first semester of college was putting enough stress on him already, so I just told him about my bruised knee.

"Two car accidents in one week? Are you sure you're okay?" Something about the way he said it made it sound like he was suggesting it was more than a coincidence, but honestly, I couldn't think of an alternative.

I plopped down onto my bed. "I knew you would worry."

"Worry? Me? Never," he feigned before his tone

returned to normal. "Of course I'm worried about you, Crystal. I love you."

My heart fluttered even though I'd heard him say that a million times since last spring. "I love you, too, Robin."

"Maybe you should just take it easy," he suggested.

"I am. I haven't even been participating in drills during volleyball practice. Coach didn't even put me in the game on Tuesday."

"You have a game tomorrow, right?"

"Every Tuesday and Thursday."

"Do you think your coach will put you in tomorrow?"

I shook my head even though he couldn't see me. "Not a chance, not until I get my stitches out next week."

"Maybe you should skip," he suggested. "I think you should take the day off and get some rest. You've been acting . . . I just think you could use a day off."

I didn't bother prodding him for what he was going to say. I knew it. I'd been acting *off*, and even though we'd only talked on the phone since my accident, I wasn't surprised that he'd picked up on it.

"It's a home game," I pointed out. "We don't need to travel or anything. It should be fine."

"Crystal." Robin's tone became more serious. "Why can't you just give yourself a break every now and then? You deserve it."

"I do?"

"Of course. I have a big break between classes in the

middle of the day tomorrow. I could come over and help you feel better."

What is he suggesting? "You mean, skip out of school? Mom and Teddy would never go for it."

"It's not skipping out of school if you're sick."

"I'm not sick," I defended, curling up beneath my blanket.

"That's not what I mean exactly, but you've been through a lot this week. You could use some rest."

I sighed in defeat. Sleeping in *did* sound nice, and if I said I was sick, I could easily get out of school and volleyball for a day. At least my babysitting job had been put on hold during volleyball season, so I didn't have to worry about that.

"I'll talk to Teddy," Robin assured me. Robin was Teddy's nephew—though we'd been dating before Mom and Teddy got married—so they were pretty close. "Besides, I miss you, and I don't want to miss you visiting this weekend. You could end up stressing yourself to death."

I giggled lightly. "I doubt that."

Robin and I talked for a while longer until he said he had to go for some sort of get-together at his dorm. Although he was only going to school a few minutes from his parents', he'd decided to live in the dorms "for the college experience," he'd said.

"Okay, I'll talk to you later," I promised. "I love you."

"I love you, too, Crystal."

As soon as I hung up, an eerie silence fell over my bedroom. Mom was still at the shop since we were getting into Halloween season, and they always stayed open later in October because of that. Teddy had said he was getting Roger to drive him to the dealership today to pick up our new car. His, he said, was old enough that it wasn't worth fixing anymore. To be honest, I think he was glad my accident gave him an excuse to buy a new — well, new to us — car, not that he wasn't worried about me. Anyway, because my mom and Teddy were busy, I was home alone.

I slipped a hoodie over my head and headed toward the kitchen to find something to eat, all the while contemplating what Robin had suggested. He was right. I *had* had a tough week. It wasn't just the pain in my head and knee, either. I had been living my week in a daze, going to bed early and not really paying attention in class. Maybe I could use a day away from school and volleyball practice. At least then I might have the time to sit down and figure out where exactly I was with my abilities.

A chill spread over me as I made my way to the kitchen, so I adjusted the thermostat as I passed the controls. I shuffled through cupboards, but I wasn't the best cook in the world, so I didn't know what to make. I wasn't even that hungry, but I knew I needed to eat *something*. Finally, I found bagels and popped one in the toaster.

While waiting for my bagel to toast, I settled into a

chair at the table and balled my sleeves into my hands. Jeez. Did no one notice the temperature outside had dropped recently and it was time to kick on the heater?

I chewed on my nails, again mulling over Robin's suggestion. It *would* be nice to see him, but would Mom and Teddy really let him come over with no one else here? No. The idea was absurd. The whole concept of skipping school and the volleyball game made me feel like I'd already broken the rules.

My bagel popped, and I jumped, looking up from my nails for the first time in the last few minutes. When I finally raised my gaze, I nearly fell out of my chair. A shadowy figure stood between where I sat and the front door. I squealed the same split second the door opened and my mother stepped through it. The figure whipped around and stared at her for a moment before disappearing.

My heart rate slowed, and I suddenly realized what the chill I'd felt was. It was because the ghost had been there. Both fear and relief flooded through me at the same time. Fear because the chill indicated the ghost had been there for several minutes. It was like he'd been watching me that whole time. Relief because it was another sign that my abilities hadn't been completely lost. I released my firm grip on the side of my chair as my mother stepped closer to me.

"What was that all about?" she asked.

I swallowed. "I—you just scared me. My bagel popped when you came in the door, and it made me jump is all." I didn't know why I didn't tell her about the ghost—probably because I still couldn't work up the courage to tell anyone that my abilities had been failing me lately, and I didn't want to explain how the ghost appeared hazy. She didn't seem to notice I wasn't telling her the whole truth.

"Yum, bagels. Can you toast me one?" She retreated down the hall to drop her purse in her room.

My hand shook lightly as I spread cream cheese on my bagel and then popped my mom's in the toaster. I shouldn't have been so frightened. I mean, it was only a ghost, and I'd communicated with several in the past year. Unlike what people tended to think about ghosts, all the ones I'd seen had been friendly. At the same time, most of them wanted something from me, like my help to solve some mystery or communicate with their loved ones they'd left behind. I'd helped them because, well, I was the only one who could.

I knew seeing this ghost meant I had to help him, too, that he wanted something from me, but I hadn't actually spoken to him yet, so how could I know what he wanted? With my hazy abilities, that task could prove quite difficult.

My mom returned to the kitchen with her phone in hand. She didn't look up from the screen as she spoke. "You left me a voicemail? What about?"

I shrugged like it was nothing. "The field trip."

"Was it fun?"

I swallowed my bite of bagel and leaned against the

counter. "It was . . . eventful."

"Oh, my gosh." She finally glanced up from her phone. "The school left me a message, too. Crystal, what happened today?"

Then I told her everything I could—everything except the bit about the ghost because I knew that would only worry her. Normally, I was more than willing to open up to the people I loved, but I couldn't bring myself to let them all worry before I even knew what was happening myself.

After my mom finished listening to her voicemail messages, I spoke again. "Robin thinks I should take the day off from school tomorrow. He says I've been through enough this week."

My mother set her phone on the counter and began spreading cream cheese over her own bagel. "I can't say that's a bad idea. You probably should have stayed home Monday, too."

I gaped at her. She liked the idea? "But I'm not actually sick."

"After what happened today, I think you deserve to relax."

"Mom, where's this coming from?"

She bit into her bagel and spoke between chews. "You keep telling me to stop worrying, and you're doing enough worrying for the both of us. Have you seen yourself lately? Two car accidents in one week is a lot to take in, and maybe you should just take tomorrow to sleep it off."

I wasn't about to argue with my mom if she was willing to give me permission. I finished up my bagel and escaped to my room to work on the homework I had to make up after going on the field trip that day. While finishing it up, I eyed the crystal ball sitting on my desk a couple of times, wondering if my abilities were strong enough to try that out and see if I could gather a clue to what the mystery ghost wanted from me. I fell asleep before working up the energy to try it out.

6

I woke Thursday to the feeling of strong hands lightly shaking me. When my eyes shot open, I found Robin's smiling face standing above me.

"Rise and shine, beautiful."

"Wh—what?" I asked, dazed. I knew I was staying home from school today, but I didn't expect Robin to be in my bedroom so early in the morning. Was I dreaming? "What are you doing?" I pushed myself to a seated position. I made a point to keep most of my body covered because my pajamas were rather skimpy— short shorts and a tank top, not that Robin would mind. "I thought you had class."

"Already done," he smiled.

"What? What time is it?"

"It's past 10." He twisted away from me to grab a

plate I hadn't noticed was resting on my desk. "Breakfast?"

I stared down at the plate of eggs, toast, and bacon curiously. "I slept in that long?" was all I could say.

"I told you that you needed the sleep." He shoved the plate toward me, insisting I take it, so I did.

"Where are Mom and Teddy?" I asked after swallowing a bite of eggs. I noticed immediately how great of a cook Robin was. I'd never tasted Robin's cooking before, but I guess he took after his uncle.

Robin shrugged. "At work."

"So, Teddy actually let you come over with no one else here? Seems to me like you're pushing your luck. I'm shocked enough that they let me visit you at school on the weekends."

"That's because they met my roommate, and he never leaves the room. Even if we *wanted* to do anything, it's not like we'd be able to find a private place short of sneaking into one of the bathroom stalls."

It's not like I didn't *want* to do anything with Robin, but it just hadn't happened yet. I shrugged. "I guess Mom and Teddy do trust us. It's not like we've given them a reason not to."

"And I don't intend to," Robin said, finally taking a seat on my bed.

"But still . . . It's hard to believe Mom and Teddy let you come over unsupervised."

"Oh, they didn't," Robin said casually.

I immediately stopped chewing. "What do you

mean? I thought you said you'd talk to Teddy."

"I did. I just didn't tell him I'd be coming over."

"Well, that's a great way to earn his trust," I said sarcastically. I couldn't believe he lied to my parents. "What *did* you talk to him about?" The question came out a bit too sharply.

"I talked to him about how you'd had a rough week and convinced him you should take it easy for a day. They don't have to know about my visit."

"Oh. I already talked to my mom last night about staying home."

Robin shrugged like it wasn't a big deal. "Well, it looks like I was right. You've been sleeping for hours."

"Then why'd you wake me up?" I teased.

"I couldn't let the food go cold." He smiled.

Convinced I needed my rest but not wanting to waste a moment of my company, Robin made me stay in bed while he brought out his laptop and pulled a movie up on Netflix.

"One of my favorites," he said, peeling back the covers to cuddle next to me. He didn't bother to kick off his shoes first. I suspected it was because of his leg. Even after all this time, he was still self-conscious about it. I had to wonder if that was one of the reasons we hadn't made our relationship physical yet—not that I was 100 percent ready to take it to the next level, either. But then again, he did manage to get me alone . . .

"Robin," I pushed away lightly before he hit play on his laptop. I twisted to look him straight in the eye.

"What are we doing? Why did you make me stay home from school? Is this . . . Are we . . ." I couldn't finish that sentence. "I'm not quite ready yet," I finally said.

Robin let out a light laugh. "Crystal, that's not what this is. Honestly, I'm just concerned about you and thought you could use some comfort."

"Well, with everything, it just seems like—"

Robin cut me off by placing an index finger to my lips. "When the time is right, it's going to be better than watching some lame movie in your bedroom."

"I thought you said this was one of your favorite movies," I said behind his finger.

He laughed again. "I didn't mean the lame movie thing like that. For real, I just—" His expression shifted to become more serious. "I just got scared, okay? It was bad enough hearing about your first accident this week, and then you told me about what happened yesterday. I just wanted to spend time with you."

I swear I saw a hint of tears welling up in his eyes. It was a side of Robin I rarely saw, so I knew everything he was saying was genuine.

"I was just scared, okay?" he repeated.

I nodded. "It's okay. I'm not going anywhere. I love you." Then I planted a long, passionate kiss on his lips before turning toward the laptop and snuggling up in his arms. After the movie ended, Robin and I lay there in silence long enough that we both fell asleep. We woke to the sound of Robin's phone.

"Sorry," he said, pulling away from me while

wiping drool off his lower lip. "I set an alarm for when I had to head back to class." He shifted to turn the alarm off. "I should go, even though I don't want to."

I yawned. "It's fine. You have to get back to class. You really did make me feel better."

A grin formed across his face. "I'm glad to hear that. Now, you keep getting better so you feel well enough to come visit me this weekend, okay?"

"I will," I promised.

Once Robin left, I felt at a loss of what to do. At first, all I *could* do was replay the day in my head and think about how comforting it was to nap in Robin's arms. I still couldn't believe the guy had the guts to come over while my parents were at work. I'm sure he knew that if he had told me to begin with that he'd be coming over secretly, I would have never allowed it. Once he was here, though, I didn't want him to leave. I wanted him right back here in my arms, but I couldn't be the type of girlfriend who made him skip class for her.

I crawled out of bed for the first time that day to use the bathroom. When I returned to my room, I noticed the plate Robin had brought me for breakfast was still sitting on my desk next to my crystal ball. I decided to take a shot at using the ball, although I didn't think it would do any good considering I'd never been very good at using it. Now with my abilities going haywire, I wasn't sure it would work at all.

After taking my breakfast plate to the kitchen, I situated myself in my desk chair next to the ball and hovered my hands over it. I was already calm enough from my earlier nap that I didn't think I needed to do any more relaxing.

I breathed in a deep breath and then let it out slowly, further relaxing the muscles in my shoulders and face. In and out. In and out. My mind fought to forget about the mysterious ghost and go into my crystal ball gazing with no expectations. Eventually, I managed to clear my head enough that my troubles seemed nonexistent at the moment. When I stared deep into the crystal ball, it appeared as if faint colors were swirling in it—so faint that I may not have noticed them if I hadn't been practicing and knew exactly what the ball looked like normally. A complete sense of serenity fell over me, but as the minutes passed, the colors failed to take shape. I didn't let my frustrations get to me.

The sound of the doorbell snapped me out of my trance.

I pushed away from my desk. Even though I couldn't make out any shapes in the ball, the fact that I'd made some connection with it left me feeling hopeful— hopeful that my abilities would return to normal at some point.

I didn't rise from my chair right away. Instead, I closed my eyes and attempted to form a mental image of the visitor at the door. It was a game Emma liked to play. It was supposed to help me practice my abilities and make them stronger. Normally, it was a simple task, but now, I could use the practice in hopes of rehabilitating my gift. I couldn't conjure a mental image of the visitor before the doorbell rang again and a voice called to me from the living room.

"Crystal, are you home?" It was Emma.

I sighed, feeling down that the simple exercise hadn't worked, but I stood and exited my room to meet her anyway.

7

When I made it into the living room, I immediately noticed that Derek was with Emma. I blushed lightly before quickly rushing back to my room to slip on sweat pants and a t-shirt over my pajamas.

"I'll be right back," I called. I noticed the clock next to my bed read 3:28. My friends must have come over right after school let out. "What's up?" I asked once I emerged back into the living room.

Emma dropped her backpack on the couch. "You were sick from school today, so we thought we'd come over and take care of you before the game."

"I don't need taking care of," I told them, but I did appreciate that they were worried about me.

Emma headed to the kitchen while she spoke, and Derek and I followed her. "It's no problem. After what happened yesterday and last weekend, I get that you may be a little shook up." She pulled a pot from the cupboard as if she owned the place, but I didn't mind. She'd spent enough nights at my house over the years that it was like a second home to her. She set the pot on the stove and pulled Derek into her arms before speaking again. "Besides," she joked, "Derek and I could use the parenting practice."

I knew her words were only in jest, but Derek immediately pushed away. "Whoa, I am not ready to hear that."

Emma poked him. "I'm just teasing."

At least he was able to laugh along.

"You don't look sick," Derek pointed out when Emma turned back to the cupboards.

"I'm not," I answered honestly, sinking into one of the kitchen chairs as I spoke. "At least not physically. I really needed the mental break with everything that happened this week."

Derek took a seat across from me and nodded like he understood. "Is it . . ." He paused for a second, trying to come up with the right words. "Is it psychic related?"

I eyed him curiously. "Did Emma tell you?"

Emma's voice piped up from across the room without even turning toward us. "No, she did not."

I gazed down at my fingernails, which had been chewed down to nearly nothing—apparently a new habit I was forming. "Is it that obvious?"

Derek shrugged. "Not *that* obvious. It's just that I've

seen you go through this psychic stuff before, and you've been acting weird, like something is bothering you — something more than your car accident."

Derek had never admitted to believing I was psychic, but with everything he'd seen, I knew his skepticism had declined over the past year. As Emma pointed out not too long ago, even though Derek was somewhat religious, he didn't have to abandon his belief system to believe me. After all, we both believed in the afterlife.

My gaze shifted between Emma and Derek, although Emma wasn't paying any attention. Should I open up to Derek? I mean, he was one of the first people I told about being psychic because I love him like a brother, but this whole losing my abilities thing made me wary to admit any of my recent encounters out loud. What else was I supposed to do, though? It was obvious — at least to my best friends — that something was going on.

I chewed the inside of my lip. "I've been seeing another ghost."

Derek gave a slow nod as if absorbing the information. "So, uh, what does the spirit — ghost — want?"

I shrugged. "I have no idea. He never said anything to me."

"I have an idea!" Emma practically shouted, flicking her mixing spoon into the air, which sent splatters of soup across the room. She ignored it and rushed over to the table and slid into the chair on the end between Derek and me. "We could . . ." she paused for suspense. "We could hold a séance."

I swallowed. Were my abilities up to that? Derek and I exchanged a wary glance, but Emma continued.

"If we contacted him, you could see what he wants and help him!"

"I—" I started to say, but Derek's voice cut me off.

"That might actually work," he agreed.

Wait. What? Derek was willing to be in on this? So he *did* actually believe me now?

My best friends stared at me expectantly. If I refused, that would look suspicious. I had to comply.

"I don't know if it'll work." I sighed. "Remember when we tried contacting Sage's sister, Melissa? She didn't appear that time." At least it wouldn't seem so bad if this time didn't work, either.

"It's worth a shot," Emma pointed out.

"Okay," I decided cautiously. "We'll try, but after soup."

"After soup," Emma agreed.

***

My friends and I formed a triangle on my bedroom floor. I had lit a few tea candles to set the mood.

"So for this to work," I explained, "we all have to be in the right mindset, which means you need to be relaxed and open to any possibilities, even if we end up

52

contacting someone who isn't the ghost I've been seeing." My eyes bore into Derek's.

"What?" he asked innocently.

"You have to *believe*," Emma told him.

"Come on," Derek said, "you guys think after everything I've seen Crystal do I'd still question that psychics are real? She found Sage bleeding to death and saved her life at the *exact* time she said it was going to happen. If that's not a miracle . . ."

"It's not a miracle, you dummy." Emma swatted at him lightly. "It's paranormal — supernatural — whatever you want to call it."

"Okay." Derek held his hands up defensively. "All I'm saying is that I believe it now."

"Okay," I agreed. "Now that we have that out of the way, let's focus on our ghost." I filled my voice with confidence, but the truth was, I was anything but confident. In fact, I was *sure* this wouldn't work. "The thing is that we don't have anything that belonged to the ghost. We don't even know his name or anything, so we'll have to focus harder than normal."

Emma's smile widened, and I knew she was fully enjoying this.

"Let's start by linking hands and doing some breathing exercises to clear our minds," I instructed.

Emma and Derek followed my lead while I guided them through relaxation exercises and continued to remind them to clear their minds of nothing but our ghost. I didn't know how much time passed. It could have been 10 minutes or half an hour. It wasn't long enough for me to give up, but then I felt something tingling my senses. I sucked in a sharp breath, and without consciously realizing it, I squeezed my friends' hands tighter.

"Something's happening," I whispered, focusing my mind even more on the mysterious ghost. What could I do to help him? What did he need?

The tingling in my fingers grew more intense, though not to the level I was used to when I saw a ghost. I took in another long breath and let it out slowly, picturing the silhouette of the shadowy ghost in my mind. A chill spread throughout my skin, raising the hairs on my arms.

Focus. Focus. I repeated this in my head, locking onto an image of the man's outline. He was almost here, almost ready to tell me what he needed my help with. The tingling sensation grew stronger, and then swiftly, my eyes sprung open. The shadow ghost hovered only inches from my nose, but I didn't have even a moment to take in the scene before the energy in the room exploded.

There wasn't a noise or a light as one might expect from an explosion. Instead, it was as if a strong, silent wind had blown through the room to whip my body back. My shoulder blade slammed into the sharp corner of my desk. I cried out in pain. When I managed to focus on the room, I saw in the dim light—thanks only to daylight behind my curtains since the candles had blown out—that my friends had been forced back from the circle as well. Emma was rubbing her head after hitting the wall, and Derek's body was pressed up against my closet door. He looked around in a daze.

"Is everyone alright?" I asked immediately, rubbing my aching shoulder. Add that to the list of aches and pains I'd accumulated this week.

"What happened?" Emma's eyes went wide. "That was *wicked*!"

I wasn't sure how far off she was with that statement.

"Derek?" I asked.

He looked at me with an expression like he couldn't really recall where he was.

"Derek?" I repeated. "Are you okay?"

He pushed himself up to a more comfortable position. "I'm—yeah." He looked down at his hands, flexing them, making me wonder if he'd gotten hurt as well.

"Are you sure you're okay?" Emma asked worriedly. She touched him lightly.

"I'm good," he assured us.

I pulled myself from the floor and flipped the light back on. "I—I don't know what happened, but I don't think I want to try that again."

Emma looked at me warily. She was still crouched next to Derek.

"Yeah," he said. "Best not."

"I think we really freaked him out," I told Emma

after Derek left to use the bathroom.

"To be honest, it freaked *me* out," she admitted. "But at the same time, it was *really* cool, whatever it was."

"I couldn't tell you what it was." Even if my abilities were working properly, I may not have been able to explain it. It was like a surge of paranormal power, only I had no idea what it meant.

8

After a while, Emma announced it was time to head to the game. She asked if I wanted to come, but I insisted I still needed my "sick" day. Emma dragged Derek from my house and went to the game without me. I was slightly disappointed that I wouldn't be there to watch it, but I wouldn't be playing anyway.

I lay down on the couch knowing Mom and Teddy wouldn't be home for a while. Mom was at her shop, and Teddy had said he'd be over at Roger's working on the baby crib they were making in Roger's workshop. I flipped on the TV to kill time. I needed something to take my mind off everything, although I really should have been working to solve the mystery of the shadow ghost. I must have fallen asleep because I jolted awake to the sound of someone entering the door.

"How was your day?" my mom asked. "Did you just watch TV all day?"

I shrugged, pushing myself up. "I watched a few things." It wasn't a lie. No way could I tell her about Robin popping in for a visit, and that sent a guilty sensation to form in my stomach. I still hadn't decided if I'd tell her about the other thing that happened. I'd been hiding enough lately. What was one more thing?

"What is it?" My mother sat beside me on the couch.

"Nothing," I told her, but she didn't buy it.

"Your face says otherwise."

I had to give her something, so I spit out the first thing I could think of. "I've just been thinking."

"About?"

"I know what I'm capable of, but I was curious what kind of powers ghosts have." Hopefully I made it sound like a simple enough question so it wouldn't prompt her to ask about the creepy encounter from earlier. I still wasn't ready to talk about it.

"Well, you're the one who sees ghosts."

"Yeah, but you know more about all this than I do."

"From what I do know, ghosts can't do much but communicate with us. That's how we get visions. The longer they've been dead, the more power they have."

I recalled the time when a ghost I knew, Olivia Owen, was able to push over a guy with the power of the wind. She'd been dead for a year at the time.

I nodded. "That makes sense. Thanks for satisfying

my curiosity."

"Are you hungry?" my mom asked as she rose from the couch and finally slipped her jacket off.

"No, I—oh, my gosh! What happened?"

A strip of gauze wound its way around her forearm. A thin line of blood was visible under the bandage.

She inspected her arm. "Dang, it's still bleeding."

"What happened?"

"I was unpacking some inventory, and I was stupid and put the box cutter on top of a pile of unstable boxes. When I bent down, I knocked the pile over. The box cutter fell on me and sliced my arm open."

"I'm glad you're okay. Now you have a wound to match mine," I teased, pointing to my head.

"It's not a perfect match, but we can grieve together. Let's do ice cream for supper."

Ice cream for supper? My mom was awesome.

***

My day off didn't seem long enough. When my alarm buzzed Friday morning, I audibly groaned as I pulled my butt out of bed and sluggishly prepared for the day. I thought about asking my mom if I could stay home again, but I needed to collect my homework from the day before and didn't want to fall even further behind in class.

I met up with Emma at our usual corner and

walked with her to school. We arrived just before the bell rang that released students from the commons and to their lockers. Everything about the day felt positively normal, like the last week hadn't even happened. I wasn't even surprised when Derek met up with us at our lockers and had to ask Emma for his combination again. He'd misplaced his class schedule for the second time in the few weeks since school had started and had to pick up another copy from the office. It was so typical that it almost felt strange to me with everything that had been happening lately. The pulse of my headache, however, reminded me that everything that had happened this past week was, in fact, real.

Luckily, my headache subsided as the day went on, but it returned at lunch. I pushed my chicken patty away from me, suddenly losing my appetite. The sad thing was, I really liked the school's chicken patties.

"You okay, Crystal?" Emma asked from across the table. She giggled and shifted in her chair like she'd already forgotten the question. Her eyes darted to Derek's, who had a blank expression on his face and didn't seem to notice. It was obvious she was trying to play footsy with him under the table. I didn't mind so much since I was used to it.

"I'm just not hungry," I told her. "My headache is back. Want my chicken?"

"Crystal Frost is turning down her chicken patty?" Emma teased.

I nodded.

"Mm." She smiled down at my sandwich like she'd just won a pot of gold. "After I finish mine."

"Want my tater tots, Derek?" I offered since they were his favorite.

An emotion I couldn't read flickered across his face, but he didn't say anything.

"Derek?" I asked a second time.

He blinked a few times before answering. "Uh, no."

"What?" Emma asked exaggeratedly. "Since when does Derek Johnson turn down tater tots?"

Derek's eyes shifted between mine and Emma's. After a brief pause, he spoke. "I just think she should eat, is all." He gestured toward me when he said "she."

"Well, yeah, but you never turn down tots." Emma leaned into Derek and clung to his arm. She looked up at him with big brown eyes. "Are you okay? You're not getting sick, too, are you?"

Derek shrugged her off. "I'm fine," he assured her before his expression changed to a more cheerful one and he fixed his gaze on me. "Do you want to hang out after school? Maybe at your house?"

"That's a good idea." I smiled. It might actually make me feel better. "I don't know what we'll do, but if your guys' parents are okay with it, we can walk home together after volleyball practice."

"Right. After volleyball," Derek said. "Sounds good."

***

Practice resumed like it had the last few days with me playing co-manager with Derek. We didn't really talk much, and I didn't mind since I still wasn't feeling well. We just ran around trying to keep the balls on the court. I was happy to see Emma kill her jump serve since it was something she'd been working on.

"Did you see how well I did at practice today?" Emma asked on the walk back to my place. She held Derek's hand and leaned into him.

"I did. It was awesome. I'm falling behind, though, thanks to my stitches," I complained.

"Oh, don't say things like that," Emma encouraged. "You had an awesome jump serve last week."

"Yeah, *one*. Most of the time, I can't make it over the net. I'm thinking I'll just practice my normal serves. I'm not sure I'll ever get a jump serve down."

Emma wrinkled her nose in thought, which made her look like a chipmunk. "I don't know. I guess do whatever works for you. You're pretty good at serving either way."

We reached my house, and I pushed inside only for the smell of Teddy's delicious cooking to hit my nose. "You're not at Roger's?" I asked as I stepped into the kitchen. The smell of garlic bread filled my senses.

"Nah, his wife's out of town for the weekend, and he had to watch the kids. We didn't want to do wood working with little ones running around."

"I hope you don't mind if Emma and Derek stay for supper." I glanced back at both of them while I spoke.

"It's fine. I'll just put in some more garlic bread. There's enough spaghetti to go around."

"Thanks," I told him before turning back to the living room.

"Where's your mom at?" Derek asked as he and Emma trailed behind me.

"It's mid-October," I pointed out. "Everyone's getting ready for Halloween, so the shop's staying open later. I never know when she'll be home this time of year."

"Hey," Emma said as she took a seat on the couch. "Maybe we should decide on a time to go shopping again for our Halloween costumes. Derek and I are thinking about going to the festival as Pikachu and Ash." Emma cuddled into him when he took his seat.

I settled into the other chair. "I don't know what I'll go as yet."

"Well, keep thinking on it," Emma smiled. "It's going to be a blast!"

My mom arrived home a few minutes later while Emma and I were discussing my costume ideas. All of Emma's ideas were so not my style, like being a belly dancer or a cheerleader.

"I'm not going as a half-naked mermaid," I insisted about her latest suggestion. "It sounds like food is ready anyway."

Emma bounced up from the couch. "Oh, good. I'm hungry."

We all gathered around and dug into Teddy's

delicious spaghetti and garlic bread.

"Mrs. Frost," Derek broke the silence.

My mother's eyes brightened when she looked up. "It's Simmons now, but yeah?"

"Oh, right. I keep forgetting."

"No problem. What is it?"

Derek looked like he had something important to ask, but then he relaxed. "Do you have any ideas for Halloween costumes?"

My mother immediately launched into the list of costumes they carried in the shop this year. I'd already heard the list, but I listened anyway in case it sparked any ideas. I liked the thought of dressing up as an over-the-top psychic, kind of in the same style of gypsy my mom dressed up as. It intrigued me, like I had one night a year to truly show off who I was, but I was also scared it would only upset me since my gift had been fading recently. Who knew if I'd even be feeling well enough in the next few weeks to go anyway? My headache still hadn't eased.

I reached for another slice of garlic bread and noticed my friends' expressions. They were both staring at my mom, completely engrossed with her costume ideas. I locked my eyes on Derek as I pulled back from the tray of bread. It had sounded like he had something important to ask my mom before, like he had changed his mind at the last second. If my abilities were working, I may have been able to scrape by with a hint as to what was on his mind, but my powers seemed pretty much useless at this point. Still, I couldn't help but wonder what was bothering him.

Derek and Emma both called it a night at the same time. Emma hadn't brought any overnight stuff, so I figured we weren't having a sleepover.

Derek cleared his throat. "Uh, Emma? Will you walk me home?"

Emma's eyes lit up. "Of course." Then she turned to me. "We'll see you on Monday. Have a good weekend with Robin and all of that."

"See you guys," I called as they left my house.

That night, I retreated to my bedroom—my headache easing slightly—and thought about how normal my day seemed. After the last week, it was relaxing for things to be back to normal, although I knew deep down that they weren't, not really. I still had the mystery of the shadow ghost to figure out. What did he want, anyway?

I sent out a short plea to my father that night, asking him to help me find answers. Then I crawled into bed and fell asleep.

9

On Saturday morning, I borrowed my mom's car and drove to the city to visit Robin. Even though I'd seen him on Sunday and Thursday, I missed him terribly. I wanted him to wrap me in his arms and tell me everything would be okay.

To some degree, I wanted to believe that it would be, but on the hour drive to Robin's, I couldn't put the shadow ghost out of my mind. Since Emma, Derek, and I held that séance, I hadn't felt that tingling sensation anymore, the one that made it feel like someone was watching me. Granted, my headache had persisted afterward, but at least today I felt fine, which probably meant my headache was just from stress and not a ghost.

But I still couldn't stop wondering what the ghost

wanted and why he wasn't interested in contacting me anymore. Had that surge of energy at the séance somehow prevented him from coming back?

I was thinking too hard. I reached over to the radio to turn it on, and then I cranked up the volume to drown out my thoughts.

I had blasted music long enough and loud enough that I was able to nearly forget my troubles by the time I reached Robin's dorm. He met me in the commons area, and I flung my arms around him the second I saw him.

"Miss me?" he asked with an amused laugh.

"Yes!" I told him without pulling away.

"How are you feeling?" He drew away from me and brushed my blond hair out of my face to inspect the stitches along my hairline. "It looks like it's healing well."

"Mom's taking me to get the stitches out tomorrow."

"And your headache?"

I shrugged. "It comes and goes. I feel fine right now."

Robin smiled and placed a kiss on my forehead. "That's good to hear."

Then he took my hand and led me to his dorm room. His roommate, Joe, sat in the corner at his desk and clicked through items on his computer. He mumbled a half-hearted greeting as we entered the room. I didn't know Joe very well and didn't know what exactly he did on his computer, whether he was studying or gaming, but I did know he was attached to the thing and hardly ever left the room except for class. I'm sure that was the only reason Mom and Teddy let me visit Robin.

We didn't stay in the room long since there wasn't much to do there. We started with a walk around the wildlife reserve next to campus before we found our way to the basement of Robin's dorm where they had a pool table.

"You suck," Robin teased before sinking his pool ball in a corner pocket.

"I'm trying to let you win," I joked back.

His brows shot up. "Is that what you're doing? You're looking into the future to see how to set up my shot perfectly?"

I forced a laugh, but inside, my heart sank. An unexpected thought made its way into my mind. I pushed it away as soon as I realized what I was thinking, but it came back just as quickly. *What if my abilities never return?* I wasn't sure I wanted them when I first found out I was psychic. Was my accident perhaps a blessing? Could this be my ticket to leading a normal life, the life my mother wanted for me?

Except, I still had a mission with the ghost. Could I abandon that? It didn't matter how much I worried or how many questions I asked right now anyway. There was nothing I could do about it. This shadow ghost was just going to have to find another psychic to help him. I didn't let myself visibly react when I realized how painfully selfish that sounded, but what other choice did I have than to let this mystery go?

Robin missed a shot, and he gestured for me to take my turn.

He'd lined up my next shot perfectly. I situated myself behind the ball and lowered my body to the pool table for a better perspective. I wet my lower lip in concentration and then thrust the pool stick forward. The ball sank into the pocket perfectly. I jumped in excitement and couldn't help the grin that spread across my face.

"That was awesome!" Robin cheered.

Though we'd played pool several times together already, something about sinking that ball felt so *normal*. Maybe losing my abilities wouldn't be so bad after all.

***

Mom and Teddy drove me to get my stitches out on Sunday morning.

"So," I teased from the back seat. "When do we get to make your next medical run?"

My mother twisted around in her seat. "You mean for the baby?"

I nodded. "For my little sister."

"You mean your little brother." A mischievous grin spread across my mother's face, and I knew she was only teasing me. "It's next week, but you know, I'm not sure I want to know anything unless there's something wrong." She turned to Teddy in the driver's seat.

"If that's what you want," he agreed, squeezing her hand. "I don't mind being surprised."

"It's going to be a girl," I said, ruining the surprise for him, although I knew at this point I was only guessing.

I returned home afterward with a new scar along my hairline. Luckily, it was easy to hide behind my hair.

Emma noticed straight away on Monday. "Oh, yay! You got your stitches out."

I fell into step beside her at our corner on the way to school. "How bad is the scar?"

"Not bad at all. At least now you can get back to volleyball practice! We can see how good your jump serve is."

"Probably not very," I admitted. "I'll just be glad to be on the court again."

"You're feeling well enough to play again, right? How have your headaches been?"

I shrugged. "On and off. I haven't had one in a few days." We reached the school just then and headed to our lockers.

Lunch was quiet on Monday between our group of three. My headache had returned mildly, and Derek seemed oddly quiet. After a few attempts at starting conversation, Emma gave in to the silence.

At volleyball practice, I was so excited to get back into things that I was the first one out of the locker room.

After stretching and running a couple of laps, Emma found her way to me to team up for other warmup exercises.

"Have you seen Derek?" she asked, gazing around the room in hopes of spotting him.

I followed her shifting eyes. "No. He's not here?"

"I haven't seen him. He seemed awfully quiet at lunch today, too. I mean, you're normally quiet, but Derek and I never run out of things to talk about. He didn't text me much this weekend, either. Do you think he's sick or something?"

"I don't know. He'd tell you if he was, wouldn't he?"

"Yeah, that's what I thought." Emma twisted her mouth in uncertainty. "I'll text him after practice."

"I'm sure he's fine," I told her, but unfortunately, I had no way of truly knowing that.

***

I returned home that night to find Teddy in the kitchen. No surprise there.

"How was work?" I asked, dropping my backpack onto one of the kitchen chairs. I only asked to make small talk.

Teddy turned from the stove and shrugged. "It was everyday police work."

"Sounds boring." I pushed my way around the counter. "Mind if I help?" I didn't typically ask to help

Teddy with dinner — I guess I was afraid of ruining it — but I honestly didn't have anything better to do.

"Sure, Kiddo."

I inched closer to the stove. "What are you making?"

"Baked chicken and mashed potatoes."

"Oh? What can I help with?"

"Mm," Teddy thought. "Can you peel and cut the potatoes?"

"Sure."

I spent the next several minutes scrubbing, peeling, and cutting up potatoes. Just when I placed the pot on the stove, the doorbell rang. Teddy's hands were dirty from the chicken, so I offered to get the door. When I opened it, I found Emma standing behind it, only something was wrong. Her eyes were red and bloodshot like she'd been crying. An indescribable pain shot through my heart when I saw the expression on her face.

"Emma, what's wrong?"

She swallowed, and her bottom lip quivered. Her silence lasted only a split second before she broke down crying and flung herself at me into a hug. "Derek br — broke up wi — with me."

I held onto her tighter once I decoded her words through her sobs. "Oh, my god. What happened?"

Emma drew away and buried her hands in her face. She didn't respond.

"Come on. Let's go to my room and talk."

I led Emma to my room, but it was like she didn't

really know what was happening. I sat her on my bed, and her shoulders shook along with her sobs. I wasn't sure if she realized I'd moved her.

I took a seat at my desk chair next to her. "Emma, what happened between you two?"

"I don't know," she wailed, throwing her body onto my bed and burying her face in my pillow.

I didn't say anything for a long time and figured it best if I just let her cry it out. Finally, she lifted her head and wiped the tears away.

"After practice, I texted him, but he didn't text back, so I went over to his house to see what was up. I thought maybe I could make him some soup or something if he was sick." She paused for a second and began picking at the ends of her dark curls. "He was like, 'What are you doing here?' I was like, 'Well, you weren't at practice. I wanted to make sure you were okay.' Then—you're not going to believe this—but he said I was too *clingy*."

Well, okay, I didn't expect Derek to come out and say something like that, but truthfully, Emma was pretty clingy.

"He's like, 'Why would you need to check up on me? You're so clingy.' I was like, 'I was just worried,' and the next thing I know, he's like, 'You're so annoying. I don't know why I'm with you. Let's break up.'"

My mouth hung open in shock. Derek called Emma annoying? But I thought he loved her!

"Wow," I finally said. "Emma, I'm sorry."

"It's awful," she cried, falling back down onto my pillow. "We've always been best friends, all three of us. Now what's going to happen? We'll never be able to hang out just the three of us again. You'll have to choose between us!"

That thought made it feel like a brick had fallen on my stomach. *Uh oh.* I was going to be right in the middle of this, and I didn't even know what had happened!

"Emma, it's okay," I assured her. "You're still my best friend."

She looked up at me. "I am?"

"Of course you are."

"Maybe you can talk to Derek for me," she suggested, sitting up in the bed. "Maybe ask him where I went wrong. When I tried to ask, he just slammed the door in my face."

I bit my lower lip nervously. I didn't want to be thrust into the middle of their relationship battles. I didn't know what was going on in Derek's head, but he *had* been acting unusual lately. Maybe he'd been thinking about breaking up with her for a while. Perhaps that joke about them having kids scared him.

"Please," Emma pleaded with puppy dog eyes. "Maybe if I know why he broke up with me, I can change. We can be together again."

A voice in my head was telling me I shouldn't do it, that I shouldn't get in the middle of this, but they were my best friends. I wanted to see them happy, to see them together.

"Fine," I agreed. "I'll talk to Derek for you."
"Thank you, Crystal."

10

For the next few hours, Emma and I talked about her and Derek. Well, it was more like Emma talking and me adding in a few sounds where I could. Teddy didn't bother us about dinner. I figured he sensed something emotional was going on here—and not just because he was intuitive.

Emma wiped at her cheeks after her tears had dried. "I'm sorry. I've been going on and on about me and Derek. How are you?"

"It's okay, Emma," I assured her. "You need to let it all out."

She took a deep breath before speaking. "I think I've said all I can right now. I just don't want to talk about it anymore. Can we talk about something else to take my mind off it?"

"Sure."

"How's your ghost?"

My heart sank. I'd hardly thought about the shadow ghost in the past two days, and it made me feel incredibly selfish. "I haven't seen him."

"Oh? Do you think he found what he wanted?"

I shrugged slowly while mulling over her question. "I have no idea what he wanted, and he never actually got to speak to me, so I don't think so." My best theory was that the surge of energy from the séance somehow slammed the door on our connection.

"Maybe we should try contacting him again. Only this time, we should get your mom, Sophie, and Diane involved. I'm sure the energy will be stronger if we have more psychics there."

I pressed my lips together in thought. That was a good idea. I mean, I'd been saying there wasn't anything I could do about the ghost and his problems, but Emma's suggestion might actually work. At the very least, it would ease the guilt knotting in my stomach after not even *trying* to help him.

"Yeah, I'll mention it," I finally said.

Emma and I moved on to more trivial conversation. It seemed to cheer us both up, but eventually, she headed home.

"What was that?" my mother questioned from the couch after I'd led Emma out the door. She turned the volume down on the TV. Dishes clinked around in the kitchen, where Teddy was washing them.

I crossed the room to sit beside my mother, a somber expression fixed on my face. "Emma and Derek broke up."

My mother's intake of breath was audible. "Oh, no. What happened?"

I shrugged. "I don't know. Derek's been acting strange lately." I paused for a second. "He was acting weird even before they broke up. I wonder if something else is going on with him."

"Something at home, you mean?" my mom asked.

I thought about it for a moment before answering. "I guess so." That's when I realized how truly self-absorbed I'd been lately. I hadn't even realized that one of my best friends may need my help. Something was clearly bothering Derek, and even though he broke my best friend's heart, he was still my friend. Surely he needed my comfort as much as Emma did.

"I was wondering about him," my mother said, her voice cutting through my thoughts.

My brow furrowed. "What do you mean?"

She shifted on the couch to sit up a little straighter. "Well, he came into the shop today after school. I didn't ask him about it, but I thought it was weird that he wasn't at volleyball practice."

"He did? What was he doing at the shop?"

"Well, at first, he was just browsing through the costumes. I asked him if he needed some more costume ideas. He said he didn't, but he did have questions about colleges. He wanted to know more about where I went, what I majored in, if I was part of any clubs, and all that."

"I don't get it. Why would he care?"

My mother shrugged. "It sounded like he was looking for advice on where to go. I know Emma's dying to go to SMU. Maybe he was wondering if that's where he should go, too."

"That can't be why he broke up with Emma," I said with certainty, only it made a bit of sense. If he was trying to convince himself to go to SMU but didn't think he actually wanted to, maybe he broke up with her to ease the heartache of having to do it when we graduated. Except, they more than a year left together. "Why is he worrying about colleges now? We're only juniors."

"Well, you and Emma went on the college campus tour. Maybe it scared him about his future."

"Maybe," I agreed, pressing my lips together in thought. "I guess that means he doesn't want to go to SMU. What'd you tell him about it?"

"I said I loved it. I told him about how I had great professors and learned a lot, and that there were always fun things to do on campus. I told him how Sophie and I started The Sensitive Society and found Diane. We've been life-long friends ever since."

Intrigue got the better of me. "How'd you come up with that club anyway?"

My mother smiled like she was happy I was interested. "It wasn't a true club that the school endorsed or anything. It started my freshman year. I was in one of my first psychology lectures when I asked the professor about people with abilities — a sort of sixth sense. I asked if he, as a psychologist, believed in that sort of thing and if so, if there was a way to explain it with science. He told me to talk to him after class. You have no idea how excited I was to learn more about my abilities. Thankfully, my grandma had taught me a lot about how to use it, but I wanted to know more about why it happened in the first place. Unfortunately, my professor couldn't give me an answer, and to this day, I still don't have a clue how it works."

"So, what'd he say to you after class?" I asked.

"He said he knew of this girl on campus who had been interested in doing some research on extrasensory perception. She was an upperclassman in the psychology department, and he thought I might be interested in talking to her."

"What'd you find out?"

The expression that crossed her face told me she had her own little secret. "Well, I learned that there were more people with abilities than just me and my grandma."

"So, the girl you met was psychic, too?"

Her eyes brightened. "She was Sophie."

A smile broke out across my face. My mother had never told me this story in so much detail before. All I knew was that she'd met her business partners in college and they formed this group called The Sensitive

Society.

"After we discovered what each other could do—that I could see bits of the future and find things and that she could read and influence people's emotions—we became interested in meeting other psychics. So we put posters up for our 'club.' That's when we met Diane."

"And she was majoring in business," I confirmed. "She was the brains behind you opening your shop."

My mother smiled like she was glad I remembered. "Exactly." In the next moment, her face fell like she was remembering something terrible. Her gaze dropped to her hands in her lap. "Unfortunately, Diane was the only person who understood what our group was about. Other people defiled our posters and wrote things like 'witches' on them."

I gasped. "Oh, my gosh. Did anyone hurt you guys?"

My mother's gaze flew to mine, and then she relaxed. "Thankfully, no, but they weren't very nice about it, especially the people who found out we were the ones in the club. We took the posters down and mostly kept quiet. People eventually seemed to forget about it."

"So, you three were the only members?" I asked curiously.

She nodded. "Well," she changed her mind. "I guess Sophie's sister, Theresa, tried to be a part of it, but she never had the gift. She left the group shortly after we started it." My mother swallowed and looked past me across the room. It was like there was more to that part of the story that she wasn't going to share with me.

I didn't manage to get a second to focus on it when I realized something. "Wait. Theresa, Sophie's sister. That's Justine's mom, right?"

She nodded.

"I remember Justine saying her mom went to SMU, too. So, you guys were all there at the same time?"

"Theresa was in my class, but she dropped out halfway through when she met Justine's dad and got pregnant."

That made sense since Justine was two years older than me and my mom had me just out of college.

"So, if Sophie was older than you, did you start the business when she graduated or when you did?"

"It was an ongoing process after Sophie graduated. I would travel the hour drive from here to SMU. I wasn't a huge part of the business in the first few years, especially since your dad was trying to get me to go on dates every Friday night."

I smiled at the thought of my dad courting my mom. I only wish I had gotten the chance to know him better. At least I remembered him well enough to know I loved him.

"Anyway," my mom said, steering the conversation back on course. "I hope Derek figures everything out."

"Me, too."

My mother patted my knee before standing. I

watched her take a few steps and noticed a limp to her gait.

"Mom," I stopped her.

She turned back toward me.

"What happened?"

She looked down at her foot like she'd just noticed the ache in it for the first time. "Oh, it's not a big deal. At the shop earlier, a crystal ball fell from one of the top display shelves, and it smashed a couple of my toes. It's no big deal."

"No big deal?" I asked breathlessly. "Mom, you could have broken toes. One of those things could have crushed your skull! You have to be more careful in the shop, especially with the baby." I rose from my seat and crossed over to her to caress her belly.

"Oh, stop fussing," she said, casually shooing me away. "I didn't break anything. I almost caught the ball, so I slowed it down. I think I'll go take a hot bath to soothe it."

"Okay," I said, but at the last second, I remembered that Emma requested I ask her about a séance. If I had any chance at helping the ghost, it was with my mom and her friends. "Oh, Mom?"

She paused and turned back to me.

I rested on the arm of the couch. "I didn't tell you because I didn't want you to worry, but I saw this ghost last week."

She twisted her lips at me like she was disappointed I didn't tell her.

"I don't know what he wants, though. Emma suggested we hold a séance to contact him." I didn't tell her that we'd tried one on our own because I knew it would make me sound irresponsible.

"I guess we can do that," she finally said. "You have a game tomorrow night, so why don't we try Wednesday night after we close the shop?"

I nodded. "Thanks."

I retreated into my bedroom, where I texted Derek. *You around?*

He didn't text back. I wasn't sure if that was because he was honestly busy or if he just sensed I wanted to talk about Emma and he didn't want to talk to me.

Eventually, I crawled into bed that night after whispering to my father, asking him to help me find strength to help out the shadow ghost and help Derek through whatever trials he was currently facing.

11

I wanted to find Derek and talk to him on Tuesday, but I didn't get a chance to before the final bell to first period rang. It was no surprise that he hadn't shown up before the warning bell since he usually didn't, but I unfortunately didn't have any classes with him until after lunch this semester. I wished I could text him as the morning announcements read over the loudspeaker, but I was never one to sneak my phone into class, so I didn't have it on me.

Knowing there was nothing I could do for Derek until lunch, I set my mind on my other problem: the shadow ghost. I attempted to formulate theories in my mind as to who he was and what he wanted from me, but I came up completely blank. I replayed everything I remembered about him in my mind, how I noticed him on the SMU campus, how I saw him on the bus, and how he had been in my house afterward. I thought back to the séance Emma, Derek, and I held and how I saw his figure in the middle of our circle before the energy exploded in the room. None of it gave me a single clue as to what he could possibly want.

In fourth period, something finally clicked. I had first seen him on the SMU campus, and then it was like he'd been following me since, like he knew I could see him and was trying to get my attention. Could it be that he was a student, or maybe a professor, and had been wandering the campus before noticing me? It was the best theory I had. Actually, it was the *only* theory I had. I should have made the connection sooner. I made a mental note to research deaths at SMU over the past few years to see if there was any clue as to who this guy was. I gave up with formulating any further theories as soon as the bell after fifth hour rang. Now it was time to talk to Derek.

I spotted him in the hall near his locker. "Derek," I called. When he didn't look up or acknowledge me, I called again as I approached him. Finally, he noticed me. I couldn't read the expression on his face. "Are you okay?" I asked once I stopped next to his locker. "I tried to text you last night, but you didn't reply."

He opened his locker and shoved his textbook inside. "I—uh—was asleep."

"Do you want to talk about it?"

"About what?" His eyes met mine before he

slammed his locker, which was the only way to get it to shut with all the crap spilling out of it. He wasn't exactly one for keeping his locker clean.

"You can't pretend that nothing happened between you and Emma. Clearly, you need a friend right now. Do you want to talk?"

Derek simply stared at me without answering, and I wasn't sure if that meant yes or no.

"Oh, right," I finally realized. "You guys probably don't want to sit by each other at lunch." I bit my lip in thought, searching for a solution. "We could go off campus to talk."

Derek's eyes lit up slightly before regressing to normal. "Where would we go? Could we stop by your mom's shop and pick up some chocolates?"

I had to admit, that did sound good. Chocolates were part of what kept my mom's shop, Divination, going when it wasn't Halloween season.

"After we pick up some lunch," I agreed. "We can walk down to the gas station and grab some sandwiches or something."

I wanted to go tell Emma that I wouldn't be around for lunch, but I suspected there'd be tension if Derek followed me to the lunchroom. Instead, I stopped by my locker to ditch my textbook. I picked up my phone while there and texted Emma on our way out of the school.

Oh, she texted back. *Will you talk to him for me?*

Yes, I told her.

"So," I started as we emerged from the school into

the October air. I tucked a long blond strand of hair that had escaped in the breeze behind my ear. "Are you ready to talk about what happened between you and Emma?"

Derek sighed like he didn't really want to talk about it. "She's just annoying."

My gaze flew to his face, but he showed almost no emotion. How could he say that about her? Okay, I guess I could see it on some level, but she was our *best friend*. You get over a person's annoying tendencies after being friends with them as long as Derek, Emma, and I had been a group. But maybe it was different actually *dating* her.

"Derek, she doesn't understand why you broke up with her. Was it that comment she made a few days ago about having kids? You know that was just a joke, right?"

Derek glanced at me quickly. "Yeah, it was that."

Except I could tell that wasn't the whole story, like he was saying it just to get me to stop asking. "Okay, so that bothered you, but it has to be more than that. Was it about college?"

"What do you mean?" He didn't tear his gaze from the sidewalk in front of him this time.

"I mean, you know you and Emma probably won't end up at the same school, and you're trying to break things off before you two completely fall so hard that you can't follow your own dreams."

"What would make you say that?" he asked, his

tone so even that he almost didn't sound like himself.

"My mom said you came in to talk to her about colleges."

I noticed a slight change in Derek's pace. "I guess you caught me."

I knew it! Even without my sixth sense, I was still a good detective. A sense of pride washed over me, but I quickly shooed the emotion away because I knew Derek still needed to talk to me.

"Derek," I tried to reason, "you and Emma have almost two years left to spend together. Why give up those two years just because you might not be together in college?"

He didn't speak for a long time. "I can't explain it."

I could tell he wasn't going to let me push it, but I tried to get him to talk anyway. "Nothing else is going on at home?" I asked with worry in my tone.

"What? No." This time, Derek did look at me. "It's just the college thing."

"Don't you want to talk about it?"

"No, actually, I don't," he told me in a clipped tone.

Luckily for him, we reached the gas station just then. I picked up a turkey sandwich, and Derek grabbed some chips and a burger. He didn't have money on him, so I paid for his lunch with a bit of babysitting cash I had with me. We didn't talk much as we made our way to Divination. We simply chewed on our food. At this point, I didn't know what else to say.

By the time we reached Divination, I had finished

my sandwich. I balled up the wrapper and shoved it in my pocket. The bell on the door dinged when we walked in.

"Crystal. Derek. It's great to see you," Diane greeted when she noticed us.

I smiled and gave her a hug. When I pulled away, I noticed the expression on her face. It was almost a wince. "Are you okay, Diane?"

She shook her head slightly, as if trying to rid her mind of a strange feeling. "I'm fine. I just have a bit of a headache. Nothing to worry about."

Her hands were still touching me, and although I wasn't as good at assessing emotions recently as I should have been, something told me she was masking the severity of the situation.

"I've been getting headaches, too," I told her. "I even have one now."

She gave an encouraging smile. "See? Nothing to worry about."

"Is Andrea around?" Derek asked.

Diane's eyes finally met his. "No. She and Sophie went out to pick us up some lunch."

Derek pressed his lips together. "Oh. We just came by for some chocolates." He pushed his way into the store and past the costumes to eye the candy by the counter.

"Diane," I whispered. "What's going on? Your headache?"

She looked at me with concern in her eyes. Then she

grabbed my arm and led me into the second room in the shop, the one that used to be another business until they'd expanded and punched a doorway in the wall.

My heart pounded against my chest in worry. "What's wrong?"

"I don't know." Her voice came out as a low whisper. "I just suddenly got these flashes. It made me go kind of woozy."

"Flashes?" I asked cautiously. "What do you mean?"

Diane could see into the past—that was her psychic superpower—but I'd never actually seen her powers in action. She fell silent like she didn't want to tell me. Finally, as if realizing she couldn't hide it from me, she spoke. "It was just flashes of memories, honestly. But it was like I was seeing them through someone else's eyes."

"Does this happen a lot?"

Diane shook her head.

"How does it work? Your gift?"

She pressed her lips together. "It's like seeing memories, but I know they're not my own."

I had a good idea of what she meant. It was the sort of feeling I got when I tried to find things by touch. I just *knew* where to find them.

"And now?" I asked.

"It's nothing really. I wouldn't worry about it." And she left it at that.

We returned to the main room. Derek's face was

still glued to the chocolates in front of him. It was like he hadn't even noticed we'd left. I passed by the rows of costumes on my way to him, fingering a few as I went.

"Do you know what you're going to be for Halloween?" Diane asked.

I shook my head. "I should get on that, though. The festival is only a week and a half away."

"Do you know what you want to be, Derek?" she asked, finally getting him to look up from the chocolate.

He shrugged. "I don't even know if I'll go."

"What?" I practically screeched. "How could you not?" Only a moment later did I realize it was probably because Emma would be there. If he was trying to avoid her, he wouldn't really have anyone else to hang out with. "Never mind. What kind of chocolate are you thinking about getting?"

"Truffles sound good."

Derek and I returned to the school, but I hadn't managed to cheer him up or learn more about what was bothering him. I didn't get another chance to talk to him, and he didn't show up for our volleyball game.

"He just quit when we only had two games left?" Coach Kathy asked in disbelief before the game started.

I shrugged. "I guess so."

A muscle popped in her jaw. "He should have come to me and told me."

All I could do was apologize, not that I really had anything to apologize for, but I hated to see Coach Kathy so upset.

12

That night after the game, I locked myself in my room and opened my laptop. I hoped to learn something more about the shadow ghost before we tried contacting him tomorrow. I started with an Internet search to find out more about recent deaths at SMU. The most recent death was of a young man, who was said to have died of natural causes, but his frame was too small to be my shadow ghost.

The second most recent death I found was of a young woman. I paused for a second, wondering if my shadow ghost could be female, but when I pictured the outline in my mind, I knew for sure it was a man. The shoulders were too broad and hips too narrow to be a woman.

I skipped over the following women's deaths and

focused on the males. The school seemed to average about two deaths per year — both faculty and students — which I didn't think sounded too odd considering the thousands of people who attended the school.

After what felt like hours of searching, I came across at least two dozen articles about different male students' deaths, but none of their photos seemed to match the outline of the ghost I saw.

How much further back do I go? I wondered. I'd never seen his clothing, and his hair seemed a timeless close cut, so I had no way of knowing if he had died within the past few years or if he'd been haunting the school for a century.

I noticed how most of the deaths I ran across hadn't actually occurred on campus. Some, I assumed, were due to illnesses while others mentioned car accidents. The only one I found that mentioned an on-campus death was about a professor who'd had a heart attack in his office. Only, he didn't seem to fit the profile, either.

Could the ghost I'd been seeing perhaps have died somewhere else? But then, what was he doing on campus? I only hoped that by some miracle I would learn more about him when we tried contacting him.

***

"So, tell us more about this ghost, Crystal," Sophie said on Wednesday night after we'd situated ourselves around my kitchen table for the séance.

I glanced around at the four women at the table: my mom, Emma, Sophie, and Diane. Teddy was back at Roger's working on the crib. Quickly realizing how nervous I must have appeared, I forced myself to relax.

"I don't know that much," I admitted. I knew so little about this ghost that I thought for sure this séance wouldn't work. "I saw him on the SMU campus when we visited, and I thought I might be able to help."

"What did he look like?" Diane asked.

I chewed the dry skin on my lip. "Does that matter? Will it help?"

She shrugged. "It might help us focus on him better."

What could I say? "Um . . . He was kind of tall, short hair, an athletic build, I guess. He was pretty normal." *Except that he was just a shadow!* I held my breath, hoping they wouldn't ask any more questions about his appearance. Luckily, they didn't. "Uh, this is probably going to be tough. I don't know his name or what happened to him."

"Well, we could all try focusing on the university," my mom suggested. "If he's attached to it, it might help create a more familiar atmosphere in the room for him."

That sounded like our only option, but I wasn't getting my hopes up too high. I mean, sure, I wanted to help him. I just didn't think I could. We linked hands around the table, and I instructed everyone to relax.

"Um . . . ghost?" I called out. I didn't know how else to address him. "We can help you."

Nothing.

I forced uncertainty out of my mind and allowed the muscles in my neck to relax. I reminded everyone to do the same. This went on for quite some time. *Deep breath in, and out. Relax. Think of the SMU campus. Remind everyone to do the same. Think of the ghost's silhouette. Deep breath in, and out. Relax.*

"We can help you," I repeated again.

Again and again we went through this cycle. *We can do this,* I thought to myself. *Deep breath in, and out. Relax.*

A tingling sensation, though small, made its way into my body. It was hardly noticeable at first. Normally, my psychic feelings were much stronger, but I was relaxed enough that I recognized the sensation. I didn't let myself get too excited just yet. I needed more energy.

Deep breath in, and out. Relax.

"What do you want? We can help," I called out again. My eyes were closed to help me relax, but in my next deep breath, they shot open as a wave of energy coursed through me.

A man stood across the table from me. He had short dirty blond hair and striking blue eyes. His body was surrounded in a bright glow that illuminated his features. Now that I saw his eyes, they looked familiar. Only a split second later did I fully register where I knew him from, and suddenly, all my memories of this man came rushing back. My mouth fell open in shock, but I couldn't manage to speak, to ask him what he was doing here.

"I don't have much time, Crystal," he said.

Tears began to well in my eyes.

"I've already crossed over, so it takes an incredible amount of energy to appear here tonight."

Is that why I saw him as a shadow? I wondered. *Because he wasn't earth-bound?*

"I need to warn you," he continued. "It won't be long before you have to make a choice. You are going to have to save three of the people you love most."

My breath caught in my chest. What could he possibly mean?

His next words sent my world tumbling down.

"Soon, you'll have to die to save the ones you love."

My hands flew to my mouth, breaking the circle. I hadn't been thinking. One moment he was there, and the next, he was gone. By breaking the circle, I'd weakened the energy in the room, and he instantly disappeared.

No! Come back! I wanted to shout, but I couldn't get the words out.

"Uh, Crystal?" Emma's voice seemed far off. "What happened?"

I blinked a few times and finally swallowed the lump in my throat. When I looked around the table, everyone's eyes were fixed on me.

"You didn't see him?" I asked.

They all shook their heads. Of course they didn't. They never saw ghosts.

"I felt something," my mother admitted. "There was some sort of energy, but I couldn't hear him, and you didn't talk to him. What happened?"

I have to die to save the people I love. That's what he had said. My life for those of the three people I loved most. I didn't have enough time to consider the concept as eight eyes stared back at me, waiting for an answer.

"I was so shocked when he showed up that I accidentally broke the circle," I lied. "I'm sorry. I just didn't think he'd show."

"We can try again," Sophie suggested.

"I'm actually really tired. That took a lot out of me." At least that wasn't a lie.

"Maybe some other time," Diane said. "You have had a rough couple of weeks."

"Thanks," I told her. I opened my mouth to speak again. I had to tell them who I'd just seen, only I couldn't manage to find the right words. I fell silent.

After we'd given up, I found my way to my room as soon as I could. I pulled Luna down from her shelf and cuddled her closer to my chest than I ever had before. I pressed my nose into the stuffed owl's head and inhaled her scent. It helped soothe my anxiety slightly so that when I raised my head, I was finally able to absorb what had just happened.

For the first time since the car accident that killed him a decade ago, I'd seen my father.

13

Hours later, I still hadn't fallen asleep. I couldn't believe my father had spoken to me. All these months that I'd been talking to him — never knowing if he was there or not — he'd been listening.

Except, what could I possibly make out of the warning of my own death? When I got the warning about Sage's death, it was because I was supposed to save her. Was that what I was supposed to do here? Only, if I survived, did that mean the three people I loved most would die? That'd be my mom, Emma, and Robin. What was supposed to happen to them? When? How? If only I hadn't broken the circle, I may have gotten my answers to those questions.

My chest compressed, and my head grew increasingly sore from the tension I couldn't hold back.

I'd already cried out all the tears I could manage. Now, my sobs only came in dry heaves. I buried my head into my pillow so no one would hear me.

"Daddy, come back. Please, I need answers." I called out to him again and again, but he never appeared. I'm not sure he could. He told me it wasn't easy for him to show himself. If he could hardly manage it with a room full of psychics, then he wasn't going to show when it was just me — and a broken me at that.

Even though he couldn't appear to me, I suspected he could somehow hear me. That brought me a slight sense of comfort until I realized I didn't know what to say to him except beg for answers I was unlikely to get. I broke out into sobs again. This time, a single tear traveled down my cheek. I watched it fall to my pillow and soak into the fabric.

"Daddy," I whispered again to the darkness. "I don't want to die."

My last words drifted off, and finally, exhaustion overtook me.

***

The next morning, a sense of dread hit me when I woke. All I wanted to do was crawl back under the covers and forget about the warning my father sent me, but it had already consumed me. I could think of nothing else as I pulled myself out of bed and headed to the shower. Even in the soothing hot water, I couldn't escape my worry. The simple math wasn't lost on me. My life for the lives of the three people I loved most. It seemed like a fair trade. Besides, it's not like dying would be all that bad. My father would be there, and I knew that once I crossed into the light, I'd find peace.

So why did it seem so difficult to accept?

A knock at my bathroom door startled me out of my thoughts. My heart skipped a beat at the unexpected noise. Mom and Teddy had their own bathroom; they never knocked on mine.

"Yeah?" I shouted over the sound of the running water.

"Crystal, do you have any idea what time it is?" my mother's voice called through the door.

"No," I told her honestly. It was only in that moment that I realized how lukewarm my shower water had become.

"You have less than 10 minutes before you have to leave for school. Didn't your alarm go off?"

It had. "Sorry. I'll be quick!"

I quickly rinsed off and hurried to my room, where I threw on the first pair of jeans and a t-shirt I found at the top of the mound of clean clothes in front of my dresser. There wasn't time to dry my hair, so I threw the wet strands into a messy bun and rushed out of my bedroom.

My mom caught up with me in the living room. "Crystal?"

I paused and turned to her, forcing my face into a

placated expression. "Yeah?"

"Is something wrong?" She drew me into a hug, and I melted into it.

For a second, I didn't say anything, but then I realized she might interpret my silence as an answer. "No, Mom," I lied. "Everything's fine. I'll see you tonight. Love you. Bye." I placed a kiss on her cheek before heading out the door.

On my walk to meet up with Emma, I questioned why I hadn't mentioned the warning to my mom or told her I'd seen my father. Surely she would help me make sense of it. Fear settled in my gut at that thought. If I told her, she'd want to take my place. That would mean I'd lose my loved ones. It was either me or them, and they'd all willingly die for me. I couldn't let them do that, which meant they couldn't know.

In that moment, I knew I would sacrifice myself for them. Pain knotted in my chest, but I didn't have any other choice. I took a long, deep breath, accepting this as my reality. Now the only thing I could do was make the most out of the time I had left.

14

I played my hardest at our volleyball game on Thursday, not just because it was our last game of the season, but because I knew it was the last game I'd ever play. I killed three jump serves in a row before the opposing team sent it back over the net and my teammate Betsy returned it but it landed out of bounds.

"You were awesome tonight, Crystal," Emma raved after the game in the locker room.

I wanted to smile, but it wasn't genuine. I did well, yes, but my heart broke a little knowing it was all over. Assuming my father's warning meant my death was just around the corner, I'd never play volleyball again.

"Just think about how awesome we'll be next year," she said.

I couldn't help it. Something broke inside of me,

and I pulled her into a tight hug right there in the locker room.

She tensed in surprise. "Whoa. Calm down, Crystal. You okay?"

I pasted a fake smile on my face and drew away from her. "I'm just glad we won," I lied, something I'd become increasingly good at over the past year. She didn't notice my dishonesty.

"Me, too."

"Want to stay the night?" I practically begged. I needed more time with her. I didn't want to leave her just yet.

"On a Thursday night?" she asked.

"Why not?" I shrugged.

Emma agreed, but my mother didn't approve when I called to ask permission. "Emma can stay the night tomorrow, but you have school in the morning. I don't want you staying up all night," she'd said.

"Fine." I gritted my teeth and hung up angrily before turning back to Emma. "Tomorrow night, okay?"

She nodded. "Sounds like fun."

Friday after school was our annual pizza party to celebrate the end of volleyball season. It also doubled as our "turn in equipment" day. Derek wasn't there like he should have been if he hadn't quit. My heart dropped thinking about him. I hadn't talked to him in the last couple of days. In fact, I hadn't even seen him in school. But I felt a need to help him through whatever he was going through. I had a feeling he'd never told me the whole truth about what was bothering him, but at the very least, I had to say goodbye.

I started by saying goodbye to Emma at our sleepover that night. I never actually said goodbye or breathed a word of the prophecy to her. I simply enjoyed her company, taking in every bit of joy I could from her laugh, focusing on the way she crinkled her nose and how that made her look like a chipmunk, and reveling in all the memories of our years of friendship.

Emma snorted and threw her head back in laughter. We were both sitting on my bed and couldn't stop laughing as we recounted stories from our past. "And remember that time when you fell face first into the mud on our first grade fieldtrip to that farm?" She giggled uncontrollably. "Oh, my gosh. Your face was *covered* in crap — literally."

"Hey," I defended. "It was really wet that day, and I slipped in the mud. At least it's not as bad as the time you peed your pants on our second grade field trip to that nature center."

Emma covered her face with her hands. "Oh, god. Don't remind me!"

I wanted to tell her about how much I would miss our sleepovers and our walks to school. I wanted her to know that I'd miss our volleyball practices and band performances. I wanted to tell her not to worry about me when I was gone, that I'd be with my dad on the other side. But I didn't. I couldn't risk telling anyone, or they'd try to get me to change my mind. I would save them no matter what.

The following morning, Emma and I made chocolate chip pancakes, just one more thing I'd miss about our sleepovers. She didn't stay long because it was her dad's weekend, and she had to drive herself and her little sister, Kate, over to his house to visit.

As soon as she left, I borrowed my mom's car and drove to the city to visit Robin like I did almost every weekend. He hugged me tight when he came downstairs to meet me in his dorm's common room.

I squeezed him back and nuzzled into his shoulder, never wanting to let him go. I inhaled his fresh spring scent and went weak in the knees. I didn't want to say goodbye.

"Crystal." Robin drew away and stared me in the eyes. "What's wrong?"

Apparently I'd been squeezing him too tight. "Wrong? Nothing. I just missed you."

He pulled me back into his body. "I missed you, too. Do you want to drop your purse off in my room, and then we can take a walk or something?"

"Sure," I agreed. I had put some thought into what I wanted to do with him on possibly one of my last days. I wanted our time to count for something, but I had yet to come up with a good idea.

When we arrived in his room, his roommate was surprisingly gone.

"Where's Joe?" I asked.

"Oh, he went home for the weekend. Said he

needed to beg for some money from his parents. You know, the whole 'poor college kid' scenario?"

I shrugged, but a moment later, I realized something. "So, that means we have this room all to ourselves?" I raised my eyebrows suggestively and closed the distance between us.

Robin rested his forehead on mine, and his hot breath warmed my face. I couldn't waste another second, not when I didn't know how much time I had. I wrapped my arms around his neck and planted a kiss on his lips.

He kissed me back and entwined his fingers in my hair. I pressed my body against his, wanting nothing more than to get closer to him, to melt right into him as if we could become one. I parted my mouth slightly, letting my tongue graze across his lower lip. He mimicked my movements in reply. When I was confident he was getting into it as much as I was, I pushed at his body until the back of his knees butted against the edge of the futon under his bunk, and we tumbled down. His hands moved down over my back and then settled on my hips. I ran my fingers through his hair and parted my lips even further. My heart hammered against my rib cage, and my skin grew hot in anticipation.

Without warning, Robin tensed and gently pushed me away.

"What's wrong?" I asked.

He struggled to work his way to a seated position.

Noticing his discomfort, I reluctantly pealed myself off of him, and we sat next to each other on the futon.

"I'm sorry," he said. "We—we can't do this."

My mouth hung open in disbelief. All I wanted was to say goodbye to him.

He gripped onto the legs of his jeans and pulled them down to adjust them. "It just—it wouldn't be right."

"What's not right about it?" I demanded. A fire burned within me, one that longed desperately for him. "What do we have to lose?"

He eyed me sideways before averting his gaze. "A lot, actually."

"Robin." I scooted closer to him and kissed his cheek. "It's just us. Right here, right now. All I want is to show you how much I love you."

"There are other ways to do it than this." He still wouldn't look at me.

I blinked a few times. He was turning me down? Did he understand what I was offering him? "Robin . . ." I couldn't find the words to finish my thought. "Why not?" I finally asked in a whisper.

"It's just . . ." He scratched the side of his face. Apparently he couldn't come up with the right words, either. "You're too young," he finally said.

"I am not. The age of consent is 16 in our state."

Robin sighed. "Well, it's just . . . there are other reasons that it wouldn't be right."

"It's your leg, isn't it?" I asked. I knew he was self-conscious of it, but this badly?

He finally looked at me. "No. Well, uh, yeah. You're right. It is my leg, and I'm just not ready."

I kissed the side of his face again. "Robin, you don't have to worry about that. I'm not bothered by it at all. I *love* you. And that's all that matters."

"I love you, too, Crystal, but there are other ways to show it."

"Not compared to this, Robin." I reached up to place my hand on his cheek and pulled his lips to mine. He almost gave into it, but he caught himself before he could fully surrender to my kiss.

"Crystal!" His voice filled the room as his arms came up to shove me away from him.

I fell back into the bunk bed's metal bars. Tears welled in my eyes, but I didn't make a noise. He still wasn't looking at me.

"Just stop pressuring me," he demanded.

I held my breath to keep from crying. I wasn't even sure what I was feeling at the moment. Guilt because I'd been pushing it? Hurt because he'd shoved me into the bars? Anger because I knew I'd die without ever showing him how much I truly loved him?

"I should go." My voice cracked, but I kept my face turned away from him as I reached into my purse for my keys and situated the strap on my shoulder.

"Wait, Crystal," he insisted, but I was already out the door. "Crystal!" he called down the hall. His voice barely reached my ears as I raced away from him.

ALICIA RADES

In the car, I let go, and the waterfall of tears struck almost immediately. I drove out of the parking lot and headed straight for home. I didn't stop crying the entire way, thinking about how that was the worst possible way to say goodbye to him. I bawled even harder when I realized it may be the last time I saw him.

When I arrived home, I thought about hopping right back in the car and driving to Robin's dorm to apologize, but a little voice in the back of my head kept telling me he wouldn't appreciate that, that he didn't want to see me. And as much as I didn't want to listen to that voice, I let it consume me.

15

Although my farewell to Robin hadn't ended the way I would have hoped, I knew there were more people I had to say goodbye to. On Monday after school, I walked the short distance to the elementary school. I spotted Hope as soon as she exited the building. She ran over to a girl I recognized from school. She was a freshman named Bethany and was Hope's temporary babysitter while I was in volleyball.

I caught up to them quickly. "Hope," I called from behind her.

She turned and smiled at me, her big chocolate eyes bright. "Crystal!" She released her babysitter's hand and ran to me. The impact of her body startled me as she smashed into my middle and squeezed me tight. "I missed you," she said into my belly.

I laughed. "I missed you, too."

Bethany eyed me.

"Hi," I greeted her. "I'm Hope's other babysitter. Do you mind if I talk to her for a couple of minutes?"

"Uh." Bethany looked between the two of us. Apparently she figured I wasn't a threat because a moment later, she agreed.

I led Hope to the stairs in front of the school and sat her down. We were far enough out of Bethany's earshot, and the other students had already fled to the busses or their parents' cars.

"What are you doing here?" Hope asked me.

"I just wanted to see you." *And say goodbye.*

"Are you going to be my babysitter again?" she asked hopefully.

"I—" I glanced toward Bethany. I'm not sure why, maybe so I wouldn't have to look Hope in the eyes. "I really want to."

Hope hugged me again.

I squeezed her back. "I just wanted to tell you how much I enjoyed being your babysitter."

"Uh oh." Hope pulled away from me. "Is something wrong?"

She had always been pretty smart for her age, and I mentally kicked myself for forgetting how quickly she caught on to my emotions.

"Wrong?" I asked. "No, of course not. Why would you say that?"

Hope shrugged. "You're acting like you aren't

going to be my babysitter anymore." Suddenly, her expression shifted, and her lower lip quivered. "You are still going to be my babysitter, aren't you? You said you'd come back in November."

I pressed my lips together in thought. How was it that she could always pick up on what I was feeling? "Hope?" I locked eyes with her in a serious gaze. "Can you feel me?"

"What—what do you mean?"

"Can you feel my emotions? The way we used to connect when—when you were with Lauren?"

She shook her head. "No. I don't see you in my dreams anymore."

Why were we ever connected in the first place? I wondered. "You don't feel what I'm feeling right now?"

"Not since you saved me," she admitted.

I hadn't felt her either, but then again, she was the only person whose emotions I'd ever felt when I wasn't touching them. "Why are we connected?" I wondered aloud. I narrowed my eyes into the distance like there was someone out there who could give me the answer. I didn't expect Hope to respond.

"Connected?" Hope asked and then shrugged. "At first, I thought you were an angel or something. I prayed for someone to help me, and then there you were in my dreams, telling me everything was going to be alright."

And then it clicked. Just like that, it made complete sense. Hope had asked the other side for my help, and they'd answered her prayers. That's why I could feel her when I was searching for her last November. I'd never felt anyone else like that because they'd never *asked* for help. When I rescued Kelli, she didn't want help. It was Olivia and Justine who'd asked me to help her. When I saved Sage from her suicide attempt, it was her sister Melissa who had asked me to help her. Sage never prayed for my help.

The tension in my heart eased. "I get it now," I said aloud. I looked back down at Hope again. "I guess in some sense, I really was your guardian angel. I will always watch over you," I promised. "I love you, Hope."

She hugged me for one last time before I said goodbye. "I love you, too, Crystal."

As I watched her walk away with Bethany, a comforting sensation overcame me when I realized this wouldn't be the last time I saw her. When I moved on, I'd still be watching over her.

***

On Tuesday, I drove to the city again after school. I didn't come to see Robin. I had another friend to say goodbye to. I nervously walked into a room full of chairs and music stands with my clarinet case in my hand. Several kids about my age were milling around before practice. Some were blowing into their horns while others were goofing off in the back near the percussion instruments.

The director stood at the front of the room next to a red-headed girl with freckles across her nose. She wore a flattering white short sleeved shirt, something I would have never caught her in just a few months ago. I forced myself not to look at the scars that ran along the inner side of her forearm. The two had their eyes locked on the director's score on his stand.

"I think we should run through this part," the girl said, pointing to the sheet music. "The percussion said they were having trouble with it."

I cleared my throat lightly, and the red-headed girl looked up. Her eyes brightened as soon as she saw me.

"Oh, my gosh! Crystal!" She rushed over to me and pulled me into a hug.

I smiled but wanted to cry at the same time. I hadn't seen her in so long. "Sage."

She pulled back and looked me up and down with a smile on her face. "What are you doing here?"

I gestured to the clarinet case in my hand. "I thought I would join your therapy group for the night, if that's okay."

"That's totally fine. You aren't looking to play in our next concert, are you? Because we could use the extra musicians."

I shook my head, but I couldn't tell her that I probably wouldn't be around to make it. "No. I just wanted to visit you."

"Well, I'm glad you did."

Sage turned to her friends and introduced us. Most

of them were younger than her, in the middle to high school range. They were all a part of her weekly music therapy group she'd started with the help of her therapist a few months back. They practiced after school in one of the local high school's band room, where the school's music teacher had agreed to be their director. It was supposed to help people like her cope with their emotions. The group wasn't huge, but so far she'd helped at least half a dozen kids recover from cutting, anorexia, bulimia, drug abuse, and similar issues. They'd held a concert a few weeks back, which Sage dedicated to me after I helped save her life.

"You can sit by Kristie," Sage told me, guiding me into a chair next to another clarinet player. I guessed the girl to be about 14, but her tiny frame made her look younger.

"I'm Crystal," I introduced.

"Oh, cool," she said sincerely. "Kind of like my name. Kristie. So, what are you in for?"

I furrowed my brow. "In for?"

"They say I have an eating disorder." She pushed brown stick-straight bangs out of her face and tucked them behind her headband. "My foster parents put me in the program."

I was momentarily dumbstruck by her willingness to share. I was about to tell her nothing was wrong with me, that I was just friends with Sage, but the truth was, there was so much wrong right now. My ability had faded to the point where I hardly felt like myself these past few weeks, and now I was here because I needed one last moment with a friend before I died — something my own deceased father warned me about. It sounded crazy. Maybe it was. Maybe the entire last year of my life had just been one big dream that I'd finally wake up from soon.

I swallowed. "You'd think I was crazy."

One of her dark brows shot up. "Crazier than compulsively starving yourself for no good reason?"

I went silent.

"Hey," Kristie said. "If you don't wanna tell, you don't have to. We all have our secrets." For some reason, her words comforted me.

I stayed after the practice for at least an hour with Sage. We sight read music together. The beautiful tone of her saxophone filled the room, sending shivers down my spine.

"You okay?" Sage asked, dropping her saxophone to her lap.

"Yeah. It's just your music. It gives me shivers."

She blushed. "Oh, stop."

"I mean it. You should do it professionally."

She shrugged. "I don't know. I like helping out the kids. When I'm finished with my degree in music, I think I just want to keep up the therapy thing. It's been really good for them."

Sage was currently living with her aunt and uncle and working at a bridal shop while she went to school. A couple of months ago, all she wanted was to get away, but after what she went through, she'd settled into her life and devoted it to helping others.

"I'm glad you've found your calling," I told her.

"You haven't found yours yet?" she asked.

I'd once told Sage I was psychic, but after she'd rejected my abilities, I hadn't spoke of it again to her. I wasn't sure what she thought about that part of me. Ever since I discovered my abilities, I knew I wanted to use them to help people. Now I wouldn't have any more chances to do that.

In that moment, I realized I *had* found my calling. My abilities had given me the warning I needed to save my loved ones—and I would. That's what my fate was.

"You know, I think I have found it," I told her, answering her question.

"Oh?" she asked curiously.

"It's . . . something I'm preparing for."

She didn't prod. It was like she'd worked with enough reserved kids to know when to let people and their secrets be. She began disassembling her horn. "Well, it's really time to lock up the band room. It was great seeing you. When do you think we can hang out again?"

I tensed for a moment. I didn't want to answer that question, not when I couldn't follow through with any promises I made. I wasn't sure how much time I had left.

"We could meet up for Halloween or something," she suggested.

"The Peyton Springs Halloween Festival is this

weekend," I told her, though I wasn't sure I'd last that long.

"Oh, awesome." She stood with her saxophone case in her hand. "I'll see what kind of costume I can come up with, and I'll try to make it."

I gave her a friendly smile, never once promising that I'd be there.

***

After visiting Sage, I swung by Robin's dorm. We had made up over text the past few days, but it just wasn't the same as apologizing in person. He gave me the biggest hug when I arrived in the common room.

He spoke into my hair. "I'm so sorry, Crystal."

"I'm sorry, too. I shouldn't have left like that."

"No, it was my fault."

I drew away from him. "No. It was me. I shouldn't have tried to pressure you."

"Really, it was my fault. I wasn't honest with you."

I tilted my head in confusion.

He gestured to a set of chairs nearby. The only other person around was a student desk attendant, but he had earbuds in his ears and was listening to music while his eyes focused on a textbook.

I sat in the chair and fixed my eyes on Robin. "What are you talking about?"

He took a deep breath and rubbed a hand over his face. "I lied to you about why I don't want our relationship to get physical."

I narrowed my eyes in thought. Where could he possibly be going with this? "I thought it was because of your leg."

He shook his head. "Not with you, Crystal. I'm not self-conscious about that with you. The thing is . . ." He shifted in his seat. "I want to show you how much I love you, too. I just . . . I don't want to risk it."

I blinked a few times, still confused. "Risk what?"

Robin pressed his lips together like it was almost painful to say. "Crystal, I don't want to get you pregnant."

I let out a laugh that was almost too loud for my own liking. "Robin, didn't you have health class in high school? There's such thing as protection."

An unidentified emotion flickered across his face. Pain, perhaps? "That doesn't always work," he pointed out.

"Well, it's pretty effective."

He shook his head. "Not enough." That emotion flashed across his face for a second time, and then something clicked in my mind.

"Robin." I held my gaze on his. "This isn't about us, is it? It's about something bigger. Did something happen to you?"

He pulled away from me abruptly. "What? No. Not—not me. I'm like you. I haven't . . . But there *is* a reason."

I sat silently, waiting for him to explain.

"I never told you about what really happened with my leg."

"It was a car accident." At least, that's what he'd told me.

He nodded. "It was. But my leg wasn't all that was lost that day." He paused like he couldn't finish, but finally, he spoke. "Crystal, I killed someone that day."

16

My chest compressed. I shot up from my seat and paced a few steps away from him before turning back. "No," I said sternly. "I distinctly remember you saying, 'All I lost was a leg,' because I remember how silly it sounded."

His gaze fell shamefully. "I lied. I didn't want to talk about it."

I still didn't understand where this was going. What had really happened in that accident? I knelt down beside him, forcing his gaze to mine. "Robin, *tell* me."

He took a deep breath, stretching out the moment of silence. It fell so quiet in the room that I could hear the muffled music coming from the desk attendant's earbuds. I let Robin take his time, and neither of us spoke for nearly a minute.

Once he worked up the courage to open up to me, the words tumbled out of his mouth. "My best friend at the time had gotten pregnant at 16. Her name was Vanessa. They had used protection, but as soon as her boyfriend found out, he left her to raise the baby on her own. Her parents weren't much help, either. I was there for her through it all. I drove her to ultrasound appointments and let her cry on my shoulder when she needed to. I bought her chocolate every time she asked. I was the first one to feel the baby kick. It was a boy. She named him Jackson."

An ache opened in my chest when he talked about Vanessa, and I knew why he never told me about her. "You loved her," I stated. There was no question about it.

He nodded, and tears glistened in his eyes. "I thought I could take care of her, you know?" His breath caught in his throat. "She found this lady online who was selling tons of baby clothes for really cheap, and she needed a ride. The baby was due in a couple of weeks, and she didn't have much for him. I agreed to take her. Well, on the way to this lady's house, Vanessa went into labor right there on the highway. I freaked out and didn't know what to do. She was telling me how much it hurt, and I was trying to console her, and I just stopped watching where I was going. I drifted into oncoming traffic and . . ." A sob broke in his chest.

"She died?"

Robin shook his head somberly. "No, but Jackson did."

It took a few seconds for me to absorb all of this. I blinked several times to keep the tears at bay. "Robin. I. Am. So. Sorry."

He went silent for several long moments before speaking again. "She blamed me. I just—I don't want there to be a chance that I'd lose someone like that again."

"Robin, that would never happen to us." Except he was going to lose me. I still couldn't tell him, especially when he was sobbing like he was.

"Now you know all my secrets," he whispered so quietly that I barely heard him. "You know why I've always been so guarded."

I'd always thought it was because of his leg, but now I knew better. I hugged him as hard as I could and told him for one of the last times that I loved him.

***

I returned home that night determined to find a way around my father's prophecy. I couldn't leave Robin.

"Mom?" I asked in a small voice. I leaned against the door frame of the master bath, where she was brushing her teeth and getting ready for bed. Teddy was in the kitchen washing the dishes after our late supper.

"Yeah?" She spoke as soon as she spit her

toothpaste into the sink.

"Can I ask you something about our abilities?"

She turned the faucet on and leaned down to the sink to spit again. "Anything, sweetheart."

"Okay, so you can see the future. Have your visions ever been *wrong*?"

She wiped a towel across her lips. "Well, sure. Remember the time I told you about how Teddy and I met?"

Some of the tension I'd been holding in my shoulders over the past few days eased. I should have thought of that story on my own. If my mother was able to save Teddy from his death, and I saved Sage, that meant I could save myself, right?

"Have you seen something?" she asked, suddenly concerned.

I shook my head in honesty. I didn't *see* anything. "No. It's just something I was wondering about." I paused for a moment. "Have you ever *not* been able to save someone?"

She stared into the mirror while brushing her hair. "Crystal, are you sure there's nothing going on?"

I stiffened, but she didn't notice. "No. I swear. So, you've always been able to use your gift to help people?"

"Oh, my god!" My mother's left hand flew to her stomach, and her right hand holding the hairbrush fell to her side. Her eyes lit up when she looked back at me in the doorway. "I think the baby just kicked!"

"What?" I shouted in excitement. I stood up straighter and immediately closed the distance between us. "Let me feel." I pressed my hand against the soft plush of her robe and waited for movement, but it never came.

"Sorry, sweetie," she apologized. "It's still pretty early, so you may not be able to feel it." She pushed out of the bathroom and shut the light off on her way. My mother let out a long yawn before crawling into bed. "Sleep well, sweetheart. Goodnight."

"Goodnight, Mom," I told her before escaping to my own bathroom to get ready for bed. Only when I lay down that night did I realize she'd never actually answered my question.

***

"Want to go out for lunch again?" I asked Derek at his locker on Wednesday before he could make it to the lunch line. I needed some time alone with him to say goodbye.

He turned to me with a hard expression on his face like he was angry about something. "I don't know. I guess. Can we stop for chocolates again?" I could sense the tension in his voice.

"That's not a problem. Are you okay, though?"

We fell into step side by side.

"I'm fine," he said, but I didn't believe him. Something was definitely up, something much bigger than Emma's joke about kids and his choice of colleges.

We broke out into the autumn sun, and I stopped him. "Derek, you *have* to tell me what's up. I can help you."

He clenched his jaw as he stared at me. His blue eyes seemed a darker shade than normal. "Believe me. You can't help me with this."

He began walking briskly, and I hurried to catch up with him. "You don't know that. You can at least tell me." If it wasn't about Emma, and it wasn't about colleges, what could it be? Was it the séance? Had we freaked him out that badly that he was forever changed by it?

"Derek," I begged. "I'm your best friend. You know you can tell me anything."

He stopped in his tracks and faced me, his expression stone cold. "It's beyond frustrating, alright?"

"What is? Derek, please tell me. I want to help." Tears began to well in my eyes. I was supposed to be enjoying my time with him before saying goodbye, but I couldn't do that when he was suffering and I didn't know how to help.

"It's not something you could possibly understand."

"I understand a lot, Derek."

"Not this." He began walking again.

For each step he took, I had to take two to keep up with him. I racked my brain wondering what this could possibly be about. Something was definitely going on at home, but what? His parents were awesome, and so were his twin sisters.

"Derek," I tried one last time.

"God, just stop it, okay? You're getting to be as annoying as your friend Emma." He didn't slow his step.

"She used to be a friend to both of us," I pointed out, becoming increasingly angry at the way he was keeping secrets. "I just want to help."

"Don't worry. Soon, this will all be over."

When we reached the gas station, I slipped into the women's restroom for a couple of minutes to clear my mind. My face burned in anger, and my headache was flaring up again in response to my stress level. Derek needed help right now, and prodding him for his secret wasn't going to do any good. Being upset at him wasn't going to help anything, either. I took several long deep breaths to calm myself. *If Derek doesn't want to open up to me, he has that right*, I told myself. What I needed right now was to simply enjoy what little time I had left with him, even if he wasn't acting like himself lately.

When I exited the rest room, I was feeling better. I grabbed a sandwich and paid for our lunch.

"Derek, I'm sorry," I tried one last time, but he didn't say anything back. We walked in silence and munched on our sandwiches on our way to Divination. It was probably better that way.

When we arrived, my mom was sitting behind the counter flipping through a catalog.

"Slow day?" I asked.

She shrugged. "It's lunch time. Everyone's out eating."

"And Sophie and Diane?"

"They're in the break room having lunch, too."

"Okay. We just came for some chocolates."

My mother smiled. "Well, I can help with that. How are you, Derek?"

He just shrugged, but that darkness in his eyes returned as he stared at my mother.

"Well," she said awkwardly. "You both like the truffles. Is that what you want today?"

"Sounds good," I agreed.

Derek turned up his nose. "I'll have peanut butter."

Jeez, he was really being cranky today. I wish I knew what his problem was. I pulled my sweatshirt sleeves over my hands and gripped onto the ends in my fists. I wasn't sure if it was because I was getting more annoyed at Derek or because I suddenly felt chilly.

My mother bent to the glass case where they displayed their small selection of chocolates. She placed three small truffles into a bag for me and three peanut butter truffles into a bag for Derek before standing and shutting the display case window behind her. In the few steps it took her to walk from the chocolates to the cash register, she somehow managed to trip. I watched in what felt like slow motion as her arms flailed and a terrified expression crossed her face. The bags of chocolates flew out of her hands, and then she was gone behind the counter.

"Mom!" I exclaimed, immediately rushing to the other side to help her up.

"I'm fine," she insisted from where she lay on the ground, but I could already see the bruise forming on the bottom of her chin where she'd clipped it against the stool they kept behind the counter.

"Mom." I reached out my hands for support and quickly glanced at Derek as if hoping he could help as well.

He stared at my mother, his jaw still clenched. He wasn't even trying to rescue the chocolates that had escaped. I was about ready to snap at him for his terrible behavior, but I refrained. Instead, I turned back to my mother, who'd made her way to a standing position.

"You have to be more careful," I warned. "You've been really clumsy lately."

She sighed. "I know. It was just this dumb rug. It caught my foot." She kicked at it to settle it back into place before brushing her blond bangs out of her eyes.

I didn't take my gaze off her as I made my way back to the other side of the counter. What was wrong with her? Had the pregnancy been affecting her, maybe making her dizzy?

"Are you sure you're okay?" I asked again, handing her the few chocolates I'd picked up from the ground.

She touched her bruise and winced. "I swear one of these days I'm going to throw this rug in the dumpster."

"That'd be too easy," I teased. "You need to hang it

outside with a sign that says, 'This rug tried to kill me.'"

My mother laughed. "Are you telling me to publically shame my rug?"

I smiled playfully. "It's the only way to make it pay for the bruise on your chin."

Her laughter grew. "I'll think about that one. Sorry about your chocolates. I'll get you some new ones."

Several minutes later, Derek and I were on our way back to school with our chocolates in hand. He didn't say anything the whole way back, but he again increased his pace like he was frustrated about something. I didn't try to push it because I knew he wouldn't tell me anything anyway. His silence brought my mood down as we walked. I slumped to my locker disappointedly because I wasn't able to give Derek a proper goodbye, and I wasn't sure I ever would.

"You okay?" Emma asked at our lockers.

I bent to my textbooks and let my hair conceal my face. "I'm fine," I tried confidently in an attempt to convince more than just her. Even though she bought it, I couldn't bring myself to believe I was okay, not when I knew that nothing about my life had been "fine" in the past month.

17

That night, I eagerly waited for my mother to arrive home from work. I lay on the couch and poked at my phone in anticipation of the sound of her car, but I wasn't really processing anything I saw or read on the screen. Instead, I was consumed with thoughts about my death. What was going to happen? And could I prevent it? At least with Sage, I had a timeline to work with. I had known when she was going to die. This time, I had nothing. All I knew was that I had to die to save the three people I loved most.

My mother arrived home late, but I needed to finally say goodbye to her the way I had with the rest of my friends. I didn't know when my death would come, but I needed one more night with her and Teddy.

"Mm," my mother said when she walked in the

door. "It smells good. What's on the menu tonight?"

I sat up on the couch. "Teddy made chicken noodle soup. It was really good."

"Well, it certainly *smells* good."

I followed her to the kitchen. "Are you okay?"

She dropped her purse on the counter and turned to me. "Of course I'm okay."

My gaze locked on the bruise on her chin. "What about your fall? Doesn't it hurt?"

"Oh, it's nothing."

"Mom," I said sternly. "Stop brushing this stuff off. Is it the baby? What if something's wrong with my little sister?"

"No, sweetheart." She reached in the cupboard for a bowl. "What would make you say that?"

"Things keep happening to you, and I'm concerned. You've been so clumsy lately." I didn't want to leave her if something was wrong.

"I'm fine, really." She opened the lid on the pot that was still warm on the stove and scooped some soup into her bowl. "So, have you decided on a costume for the festival yet?"

I knew she was only trying to change the subject, but I figured it best to enjoy what little time I had left with her instead of fighting about whether she was okay or not.

"I don't know yet," I told her. I wasn't even sure if I'd make it until Saturday. "Mom, can we . . ." I trailed off because I wasn't sure how to finish that sentence. I wanted to do something with her, to make my time with her count, but I didn't know what to do.

She leaned against the counter and took a spoonful of soup. "Can we, what?" she asked once she swallowed.

I relaxed. "Can we make brownies?"

She smiled back at me.

Teddy joined us after my mom finished her soup, and he guided us through the recipe for homemade brownies. They weren't the kind my mom always made from a box. We had to use cocoa powder and flour and everything. We chatted and laughed, and thanks to Teddy's skill, the brownies came out without crusty edges like my mom normally made them.

All the fun I had with them nearly made me forget about how little time I had left. At least, I could only assume I didn't have much time left. Otherwise, why would the warning have come now? I contemplated this as I lay in bed that night. If I made it until Saturday, I'd have at least one more night to say goodbye to everyone since they'd all be at the festival.

And that's when it hit me. Everyone would be there, everyone I loved. It was supposed to happen then. My heart sank, and though I'd been full on brownies just moments ago, an empty feeling opened up in the pit of my stomach. On Saturday night, I was going to die.

***

The following day at school passed by hazily as I contemplated what it all meant. The three people I love most—my mom, Emma, and Robin—would all be at the festival on Saturday, and I was supposed to die to save them from . . . from what? The most dangerous thing at the festival would be tripping on a root along the haunted trail. What could possibly happen to them?

By the time lunch rolled around, I still hadn't come up with any good ideas. I sat by Emma, but Derek was nowhere to be seen. Emma and I chatted, and I put on a smile in hopes of making one of my last lunches with her a bit more memorable. She didn't talk about Derek, and I didn't bring him up. I only hoped they would work it all out when I was gone.

When I was gone . . . Why did I have to go? I only thought about it more and more as the day wore on. If I had to die to save three people, then it would be safe to assume they'd all be in the same place at once. Maybe if I could keep them all apart, nothing bad would happen to them.

***

"Hi, Sophie," I greeted when I entered Divination after school. A couple of younger kids were browsing through costumes nearby, but there weren't many left since it was so close to Halloween.

She looked up from behind the counter. "Hi, Crystal."

"Where's my mom at?"

"She and Diane are in the back organizing some stuff that Tammy and Sheryl asked us to bring for the festival. Need help with anything?"

I smiled reassuringly. "No, I'm good." I passed by the front counter and headed toward the storage room.

"Oh, I can use that in my tent," my mom said to Diane, grabbing the table cloth from her hands. She looked up and noticed me. "Crystal."

"Hi, Mom."

"What's up?" She pulled herself from the floor and dusted off.

I shrugged. "I just wanted to talk to you. Is that okay?"

"Sure, sweetheart. What is it?"

I glanced at Diane on the floor. "Diane looks busy. Can we talk in the break room?"

"Sure." My mom followed me across the hall to the small room where they kept their purses and snacks. A table with four chairs around it sat in the middle of the room.

I turned back to my mom and crossed my arms over my chest when the door clicked shut. "Mom, I need to know something, and I don't want you to lie to me this time."

"Lie to you?" she asked innocently. "I wouldn't lie to you, sweetie."

I chewed the dry skin on my lip because I wasn't sure exactly how to confront her about this. "Mom, the last time I asked you this, you completely diverted the question, so please be honest with me." I took a deep breath. "Have you ever *not* been able to help someone?"

Her brows shot up. "You want me to be honest with you? Then you're going to have to be honest with me." Her tone softened. "Crystal, what is this about?"

I swallowed hard, but it felt like trying to force needles down my throat. I had to lie to her. If I told her the truth, she'd want to take my place. Everyone I loved would die for me, and I couldn't let them do that. "Mom, I need you to trust me when I say that I can't tell you, okay?"

She bit the inside of her cheek. I wasn't sure if it was because she was disappointed or because she was thinking hard. "I don't like this." She crossed her arms over her chest and pursed her lips. "Can't you trust me enough to tell me?"

"It's not like that, Mom. I *do* trust you."

Her voice rose slightly. "Then why can't you tell me what's wrong with you? You're my daughter, and I'm supposed to protect you. How can I do that when I don't know what's wrong?"

And how can I save myself when I don't know how I'm going to die?

"Please believe me, Mom," I begged. "It will put people in danger if I tell you."

Her nostrils flared, and her breaths grew shallow. She took a deep breath to calm herself. "Okay. You really want to know if I could save everyone? The answer is no, I couldn't. Please, take a seat." She gestured to the break table, and I slid down in the chair farthest from the door. "Excuse me for a minute."

I didn't ask why she had to leave the room, but she came back a couple of minutes later with Sophie and Diane in tow.

"Uh, don't you have customers out in the shop?" I asked. My heart thumped in my chest nervously. What was so important that they all needed to be in here at once?

"We closed up early," my mother answered.

"But it's so close to Halloween! You can't close up."

"This seemed more important," my mom said.

She took the seat across from me while Sophie and Diane sat in the chairs on either side.

My mother shifted in her chair. "I asked Sophie and Diane in here to help me tell the story."

I blinked a few times. "Uh, okay. Why?"

They all exchanged a glance, but my mother was the one who spoke. "Because the story has to do with all of us. We were all there. We all watched Sam Marshall die."

18

"Who's Sam Marshall?" I shifted my gaze between all of them. They swallowed in unison like they had all suddenly formed a lump in their throats. My pulse quickened in response.

"We knew him in college," Diane explained.

"He was a friend of your father's. He was also my sister Theresa's boyfriend," Sophie clarified.

I drew in a sharp breath. "Oh, my gosh. Justine's mom's boyfriend?" It took me a second to absorb the information. Did that make Sam Marshall Justine's father? I'd never met her dad, but I thought her parents were still together. Plus, Justine's last name was Hanson, not Marshall. Apparently my question was written in my expression because Sophie quickly clarified.

"He was her boyfriend at the time. Justine's dad came into the picture later."

I hadn't realized how quick my pulse had become, but it returned to normal once Sophie explained. "Is that why she dropped out of college? Because her boyfriend died?"

Sophie shook her head. "No. This happened about a year before she dropped out."

My mother spoke next. "I met Sam shortly after I met Sophie and then her sister, Theresa. It wasn't long after we formed our Sensitive Society group. Ever since I met him, I kept having visions of his death, how he was going to get hit by a bus while on his bike."

My eyes widened. That must have been terrible for her.

"I couldn't feel anything strange from him," Sophie said, "and Diane couldn't see anything from his past out of the ordinary. Your mom was the one who could see his future, but we were there to support her 100 percent."

I drew closer to the table, completely engrossed in their story.

Diane took over. "We invited him to my dorm room one night to warn him about it. We thought maybe if he didn't ride his bike around anymore, it wouldn't ever happen."

"But it did," I finished for her.

My mother nodded. "The hardest part wasn't telling him that we were psychic. It was warning him of his death."

Sophie rested her elbows on the table and leaned closer to me. "At first when we told him we were psychic, he just kind of scoffed. He said he saw the posters around campus and thought our 'little joke' was kind of funny."

"We tried to tell him we were serious," Diane continued, "but he didn't believe us. I remember him asking, 'And why should I care?'"

My mother swallowed hard. "And that's when I told him about his death. I told him I'd seen it and that if he didn't trust us, he was going to die."

The surface of my skin began to heat. My mother had told me about how people had rejected her and her abilities before. A boyfriend in high school had told everyone she was a witch, and she had to transfer schools. This was another one of those stories, I knew, and she was finally giving me the details. I couldn't bear to think about all the people who had rejected her throughout the years.

"Then what?" I asked.

"He freaked," Diane answered. "He told us it was true what everyone was saying, that we were all witches."

My breath caught in my throat. I couldn't believe what they'd been through.

Sophie spoke. "I think he was more scared than anything. I'm not sure if he really believed we were witches, but we certainly freaked him out."

"He just kind of ran after that," my mom told me. "We chased after him. I remember calling out to him and asking him to trust me, but he just kept running down the hall and out of the building. When we made it out of the dorm hall, he had already grabbed his bike from the bike rack next to Diane's dorm, and he was riding away. We chased after him, and that's when it happened."

Her eyes glistened with tears. When I glanced around the table, I realized they were all on the brink of crying.

Sophie stared into the distance, not really looking at anything. "He was so scared. He wasn't watching where he was going. He crossed the street just as the city bus was coming down it. We rushed over to him, but it was too late to do anything."

Silence settled over the room until my mother's whisper cut through it. "I watched him take his last breath. I held his hand while he died."

I wanted to cry, but nothing came out. How did my mother handle her abilities after that? Everything I'd gone through over the past few weeks now seemed trivial in the grand scheme of things. Except, if they couldn't save Sam, then would I be able to save myself?

"I don't get it," I said. "If Sam only died because he was running away from you, wouldn't that make it a self-fulfilling prophecy?"

My mom shook her head and gazed down at her hands. "It wasn't like that, exactly. In my visions, it always happened a different way. He was wearing a different shirt, and the bus number was different. I remember thinking the same thing, but after looking at it all closer, I realized his real death wasn't the same one I was seeing in my visions."

"It's like he was always meant to die that way," Diane told me. "It almost didn't matter if we told him or not because he'd always end up getting hit by a bus one way or another."

My head hurt thinking about it. I didn't understand how I could save Sage from her death but they couldn't save Sam. If Sage was supposed to die from suicide several months ago, did that mean she would die from suicide later? If I didn't die this Saturday, would I end up dying later on to save the people I loved?

I voiced my thoughts. "Why can we save some people from death and not others?"

They all sighed in unison as if collectively agreeing this was a difficult question to answer.

Sophie was the first to compose herself. "Sometimes we're *supposed* to save them."

"I don't get it," I complained again. "If we're supposed to save the people we're led to, then why would Mom have a vision of Sam in the first place? Doesn't that mean she was supposed to save him?"

"Not necessarily," my mother pointed out. "Sometimes the things we see don't mean anything at all. Maybe my visions of Sam weren't even meant for me."

Though it was difficult to wrap my head around, I understood on some level. Sometimes I knew people's secrets without even caring about the answer, but I'd never seen something so *huge* without being able to help.

"Or maybe it wasn't even about his death," Diane said.

I cocked my head. "What do you mean?"

"Maybe it wasn't about saving him. Maybe it was about teaching *us* something. We all became very close after that day. We learned a lot about keeping our secrets . . . well, secret."

My mother reached across the table and rested a hand on mine. She spoke soothingly. "Crystal, I'm sorry if that's not the story you wanted to hear."

I wiped a stray tear from my eye. "No, it's okay. I think that's exactly what I needed to hear."

I left the break room mulling over their story again. My dad's warning wasn't about my death and how I could prevent it. It was about my loved ones' deaths and how I could *save* them. I had around 48 hours left of my life—if I was right about this all happening at the festival—and I was going to make it count.

I passed by the costumes on my way out, and one caught my eye. I finally knew what I was going to dress as for Halloween.

19

"Crystal, can I be honest with you?" Emma asked at lunch on Friday.

I looked up from my pizza. At least we were having something tasty on one of my last days. "Sure." Though I was dreading what was to come, I spoke confidently. There was no point in making my last few hours miserable or causing others to worry about me.

Emma shifted in her chair. "I've been feeling . . . strange."

I stopped chewing. "Strange? What do you mean?"

She shrugged. "I'm not sure I can explain it. We haven't done our psychic practice sessions in a while, so maybe I'm getting rusty, but I think I'm feeling something. Maybe it's a bad omen?"

Through Emma's practice, she'd become talented at

feeling good or bad about a situation since everyone had some intuition. My abilities had been so weak lately that I'd almost forgotten there was a chance she could pick up on my bad vibes.

"I'm sure it's nothing," I lied to her. It was the only option I had. "It's probably just about your breakup with Derek. Are you second guessing going to the festival?"

"You think he'll be there?"

I forced a look of uncertainty on my face, even though I knew he said he probably wouldn't come. It was the best way to distract her from trying to weed the truth of my prophecy out of me. "He might be."

She looked down at her food. "Maybe I can just avoid him, unless you were planning to hang out with him."

"Don't be silly," I told her. I still felt bad that I hadn't been able to give Derek a proper goodbye and figure out what was wrong with him, but I didn't know what else to do when he wouldn't talk to me about it. "If you come, then I'll hang out with you."

If you come . . .

The words echoed in my mind. What if there was a chance she didn't come? Then the three people I loved most wouldn't be in the same place at the same time, and I might have a chance of preventing whatever was supposed to happen. Unless whatever it was wasn't supposed to happen tomorrow night . . .

Make up your mind, Crystal, I scolded myself. *Are you*

going to die for them or not?

I would. I would die for them *if* I had to. But what if it never came to that? What if keeping them apart was how I saved them?

"Maybe you're getting sick," I suggested. "If you're getting sick, you probably shouldn't come to the festival. You don't even have a costume, do you?"

Emma's face fell. "You're right. It's probably just a mixture of heartbreak and the flu or something."

"I think maybe you should go home and get some rest over the weekend."

"I *do* feel kind of sick," she admitted.

Except I knew it wasn't the flu. She could tell something bad was coming. She just didn't know what her intuition was telling her.

"Well, go ahead and rest over the weekend, okay?" I said.

***

After school, I returned home and killed time by completing my homework. I wasn't sure if it would matter, though. After Teddy arrived home, I told him I was going on a walk, and I strolled the few blocks to Divination. I knew my mom wouldn't be around, but I double checked anyway.

"Is my mom here?" I asked Sophie after waiting for her to check out a couple of customers.

"I'm afraid not. She's attending a last-minute

festival meeting for us." Sophie checked the clock on the wall. "She should be back in under an hour if you're looking for her."

"No. It's okay. I was just wondering." I glanced over at Diane, who was helping a young boy pick out costume makeup. My heart sank. If something was going to happen, I still had to say goodbye to Sophie and Diane, but I didn't know how. I turned back to Sophie. "I still don't have a costume."

"Oh, that's no problem. Let's see what we have." She came around the side of the counter.

There weren't many costumes left on the racks since the Halloween festival was tomorrow, but the costume I had my eye on yesterday was still there.

"Let's see," Sophie mused. "What do we have that will fit you? I think there's still a pumpkin costume."

I wrinkled my nose as she held it up. "Do I have to stuff it?"

She laughed back at me. "I suppose you could. Balled up newspaper works well, and there's a string at the bottom where you can pull it tight so the stuffing doesn't fall out."

I reached for the costume. It might at least be fun to try it on, even if I didn't want it. "Well, let's see what it looks like."

I hurried into a dressing room and pulled it on over my head. When I emerged, Diane was done attending to the customer, and I had both of their attention. When they spotted me, they both burst out laughing.

"This is why it's still on the rack," Diane joked. "No one wants to be caught dead in that thing."

"So, why'd you stock it?" I teased back.

"You'll have to ask your mother," she responded. "That one was her idea."

I twirled around, showing off the awful costume. "Let's try the next one."

Diane and Sophie put me in a banana costume next, followed by a dress designed to look like a Skittles bag.

"What's with all the food?" I asked with a laugh.

"That's all we have left!" Sophie defended. "All the good ones are gone."

I knew that wasn't true, but I was enjoying dressing up for them. We made it through another half dozen costumes and another half hour of laughing together before I finally mentioned the costume I had my eye on.

"Oh, I didn't realize we still had that one," Diane said. She strolled down the aisle and pulled it off the rack. "It looks about your size. Go ahead and try it on."

I did, and it hugged me perfectly in all the right places as if it was tailor made for my body. When I stepped out of the dressing room, Diane and Sophie both whistled at me.

"You like it?" I asked.

"It's perfect," Diane raved.

"It looks great," Sophie agreed.

I checked the price tag and breathed a sigh of relief that I had enough cash to buy it. "Thanks. I like it, too."

I retreated into the dressing room and placed the

costume back on its hanger. When I exited the dressing room, I walked over to the checkout counter, and Sophie rang up my total. I left Divination that night both happy about my costume and comforted by the fun time I'd just had with the two women who were like the aunts I never had.

***

After I arrived home, I called Robin. I'd already convinced Emma to take it easy and skip the festival, but just as reassurance, I didn't want Robin there, either. If I was right and this was when it was supposed to happen, I didn't want any of the three people I loved the most to be near each other.

"What are your plans tomorrow?" I asked him.

"I was going to come over early and head to the festival with you. You're going to love my costume."

He still hadn't told me what he was going to be, and I hadn't bothered mentioning my costume idea, either. My eyes fell on it in my open closet, but I tore my gaze away so I could focus on the conversation Robin and I were having.

"It's not even going to be that fun," I lied.

"What do you mean? It's Halloween. Of course it'll be fun."

"Well, I'm going to be helping out with some of the booths, so you won't even see me much." It was a lie. I was going to help with the setup, but other than that, I'd be free to enjoy the rest of the night with him. But keeping everyone apart was the best option. Then nothing bad would happen to all of them at once.

"What booths are you helping with?" he asked. "Maybe I can volunteer, too."

I tried to think of a booth that would be half believable. I couldn't tell him I was working the kissing booth, but maybe he'd believe I was helping at the apple bobbing booth. "I'll be all over the place," I finally said. "I'm going to be pretty busy."

"Well, maybe I can meet up with Emma and Derek while you're working. Surely you can take a break and spend some time with us for a bit."

I swallowed hard. This wasn't working. "Emma and Derek broke up, remember?"

"Right. Well, I mean, I'll find someone to hang out with while you're busy. And if all else fails, I'll just listen to the band they're getting to play."

I could only see one way out of this. It was the only way to be *sure* nothing would happen tomorrow.

"Robin," I said sternly. The tears were already rising to my eyes, but I kept my voice steady. I couldn't risk him knowing how much the words would hurt me. I paused for a moment because I knew what I was going to say next would tear me apart, but I quickly worked up the courage. It was my only option to ensuring we'd all be safe, at least for now. "I don't want you to come."

The words sounded like they were coming from someone else's mouth. How could I possibly say something like that to him? Before he had a chance to speak, I reminded myself that if I could get past Saturday without anyone getting hurt, Robin and I would have plenty of time to make up.

"You don't want me to come?"

His words felt like a punch to the gut, but I didn't let my voice waver. "Please don't come."

"Why not?" His voice was so small, so injured. "Is this about the fight we had recently? I thought we made up."

I pressed my lips together, hoping to hold back the tears. I couldn't believe what I was saying to him, but I had to stick to my lie. "I'm not over it yet."

"I don't get it. What happened since we last saw each other? Why are you mad at me again?" He spoke slowly, each word ripping open my heart even more.

"I never stopped being mad at you." My voice almost cracked, but I forced it to remain strong. I reminded myself that hurting him now was better than walking to my own death and leaving him. It would tear him apart, and maybe, just maybe, I could spare him the heartbreak while saving myself in the process.

"Oh," he said softly. "I didn't realize. I guess I'll give you your space."

I hung up without even saying goodbye and then threw myself into my pillow. My shoulders heaved as I drowned the pillow in sobs. At least it muffled the noise so my mom and Teddy wouldn't hear.

After getting ready for bed, I whispered to thin air,

hoping my father would hear. If he had heard me before, I had faith that he'd hear me now. I asked him for a sign so I'd know if I was making the right choice. Was it supposed to happen at the festival anyway, or was I focusing on the wrong event? Did I do the right thing by convincing Emma and Robin to stay away, or was I only ruining my relationships with them?

By the time I fell asleep, I still had no idea if I had made the right choice.

20

The day of the festival arrived, and I couldn't quite tell what I was feeling. It was neither good nor bad. I didn't know what else to do about it all, so I figured I'd just take the situation as it came. To keep myself busy, I headed down to the park with my mom to help them set up. Volunteers hustled around the area, setting up the booths they were running while others headed into the neighboring woods to finish up the last touches on the haunted trail. A large stage stood as the highlight of it all, where a band would be playing later on in the night.

I started by helping my mom set up her booth. It wasn't much. We put up her tent together and then carried in her table, chairs, and props. I situated her tablecloth and electric candles on the table before adding her final center piece, a crystal ball. My mom didn't do real crystal ball readings at the festival — that was just for show — but she did give real tarot card readings.

"Is that it?" I asked, looking around the tent to see if we'd missed anything.

"It looks like it," she replied. "The only thing left is for me to get into my costume, but we have plenty of time. There are lots more booths we can help set up." She pulled the tent flap aside for me.

We spent the rest of the morning helping where we could. I spent some time assisting Sophie for a while before helping Diane. After lunch, which was provided for the volunteers, Mom and I took a short break to head home and get into our costumes.

I didn't apply any more makeup than normal, but when I looked into the mirror after putting on my costume, complete with black tights and Mary Jane heels, it felt like I'd been transformed. I never really thought black was my color, but in this outfit, with its blue accents that complemented my eyes, it suited me. The top was modest, but the tutu skirt supplied just enough of a sexy flare. I let my long hair fall over my shoulders and added the final touch: a black pointed hat.

When I stepped into the doorway of my mom's bathroom, where she was applying her makeup, she gasped. She paused and caught my eye in the mirror. "Where'd you get that costume?"

I twirled around to show it off. "Sophie sold it to

me. I think it suits me." I also knew exactly what my mom thought about it, and she wasn't pleased.

She pressed her lips together and turned to me. "Why would you want to be a witch for Halloween?"

I didn't let her discomfort bother me. "I know you've been hurt by the term before, but I guess this is my way of embracing who I am."

"Crystal, you're not a witch. You're a psychic."

A shred of guilt eased its way into my heart. I didn't choose the costume to hurt her. "But if this is the way other people see me, I don't want it to bother me. I can do things that no one can explain. In some ways, it does seem like magic. And this," I gestured to my costume, "is me telling the world that it doesn't matter what they say. I love myself for who I am." *Even if I may never get my abilities back*, I thought to myself.

My mother didn't say anything as she pulled me into a hug. I stiffened in surprise before relaxing into it.

After about a moment, she finally spoke. "Crystal, I am *so* proud of you." She drew away to look me in the eyes. "I would have never acted the way you do when I was your age. You're beyond your years. Don't ever change."

I smiled at her in response.

***

When we returned to the park, there weren't many cars around since the festival hadn't officially started yet.

"Well, I'm going to go get situated in my tent," my mother announced. "Things will get bustling here pretty quickly."

I glanced around. I didn't have any volunteer ideas in mind, and it's not like I had anyone to hang out with when I'd convinced my friends not to come.

"I guess I'll just wait around until I see someone I know," I told her.

"Okay, have fun." She waved and then headed off toward her tent.

I scanned the area for a moment and then decided to sit at the picnic tables by the food. On my way there, I spotted Teddy in his police uniform. He had just said goodbye to one of the volunteers he was talking to when I approached him from behind.

"You're not working at the station this year?" I asked to get his attention.

He turned to me, a smile on his face. "Nope. Most of the town is going to be here tonight, and they wanted two of us patrolling the festival."

"So you got stuck on duty?"

He shrugged. "I don't mind."

"Well, have fun," I told him before making my way to the picnic tables. He headed in the opposite direction.

I took a seat and again glanced around. Without my friends here, it was going to be a boring night, but at least no one would get hurt. Since I didn't have anything else to do, I pulled out my phone and scrolled through it mindlessly. After nearly 20 minutes of sitting there bored out of my mind, a shadow crossed my table. I looked up to find Justine and Kelli standing above me. Kelli wore a short red dress with a crimson hood over her head, and Justine was dressed as a sexy scarecrow.

"Hey!" I greeted enthusiastically. I hopped up to give them both a hug. "How are you guys?"

"We're great," Justine answered. "How have you been?"

What could I say to that? "I've been fine," I told her vaguely.

"Your costume is so cute," Kelli complimented.

I glanced down at my dress. "Thanks. Yours are both cute, too. So, any plans for the night?"

Justine elbowed Kelli playfully. "Kelli's volunteering for the kissing booth this year. I'm starting at the apple bobbing booth, and then I'm helping with the ring toss. Then we have the rest of the night free."

"I've been here all day helping set up, but I didn't volunteer to run any booths." At the time they were taking volunteers, I'd thought my friends would be here to spend the night with me.

Justine glanced around. "Where's everyone else? Emma? Derek? Is your boyfriend coming?"

I shook my head and opted for the easiest answer. "They were all busy tonight."

"Well, if you need some company, you can help me run my stations," Justine offered.

I smiled. "Thank you."

"Hey," Kelli said, "maybe we can meet up after we're done volunteering and we can go through the haunted trail together."

We all agreed that was a good idea, but eventually, Kelli went her own way while I trailed behind Justine and told her about Emma and Derek's breakup.

"That sucks," she said. "They made a cute couple."

Throughout the next few hours, I hung by Justine. She seemed to know everyone around, even the people I didn't know from neighboring towns. In the last 10 minutes of Justine's scheduled time at the ring toss booth, I spotted red hair in the crowd.

"I'll be right back," I told Justine before heading toward Sage. She wore an orange and white dress with matching pointed ears. "You made it! And as a fox. You look cute!" I pulled her into a hug.

She drew away from me with a smile on her face. "Thanks! So, are you working?"

I glanced back at Justine at the ring toss booth. She was smiling and handing out rings to small children. I turned back toward Sage. "No. I was just hanging out with a friend. She's almost done."

"Oh. Where's everyone else?"

Again, I went with the easy answer. "They were all busy."

She tilted her head in question. "I thought Robin was coming."

"Something came up. Anyway, we're headed down the haunted trail in a few minutes if you want to come."

"I'd love to!" Sage bounced on her toes in excitement.

We made our way back to Justine's booth and waited a few minutes for the next volunteer to come and take her spot.

"I asked a few friends to come along with us," Justine told me once she was done with her shift. "I hope you don't mind."

"Not at all," I answered as we walked toward Kelli's booth.

"It's great seeing so many people from high school again. It seems a lot came back for the weekend." Justine waved at another person she knew.

"Well, you know, our town's Halloween festival is kind of a big deal," I joked.

We met up with Kelli and then found a couple of Justine's friends.

"I'm scared," Sage faked, grabbing my elbow on our way to the entrance of the haunted trail. We followed behind Justine and her friends, with Sage and me in the back of the group.

"Oh, relax. It's just volunteers in costumes," I laughed.

"Hey, sometimes you can't tell the difference between zombies and kids in makeup. I've seen enough of those shows, and the effects are creepy."

"Don't worry. I won't let any zombies get you. I can't make any promises about the vampires, though."

Sage giggled. "I'd take care of the vampires, but I

left my stakes at home."

We made it through the haunted trail unscathed, though we all jumped a few times. When we emerged from the trees, our group split up. Sage and I headed toward the aisles of booths to explore the games. On our way, I spotted curly dark hair I recognized all too well.

"Emma!" I practically shouted in surprise before we even met up with her. She was dressed in Gryffindor robes and noticed me making my way to her. "What are you doing here?" I asked as soon as I was close enough. "You're supposed to be sick!"

She shrugged. "I feel fine, honestly. I changed my mind about coming. I couldn't sit around at home knowing all this fun stuff was going on without me." She gestured around to the games around us. "I think it's silly for me to shut down just because Derek broke up with me. I can't let him control me like this. Besides, my mom and sister were coming anyway, and I figured, why not?"

Honestly, I was proud of her for realizing that moving on was the best option, but why couldn't she have figured this out tomorrow? At least if Robin stayed away, things should still turn out fine, I hoped.

Except that before I had a chance to respond to Emma, my hopes were instantly shattered. Sage tapped me on the shoulder and pointed. I followed her gaze and noticed a pirate with a peg leg walking toward us.

My face grew hot in worry. "Robin! You—you weren't supposed to come." My eyes shifted between

Robin and Emma. Neither of them were supposed to be here. This couldn't be happening.

"I couldn't stay away." He stopped so close to me that I could feel the heat radiating off his body.

I worried that perhaps he could hear my heart hammering against my rib cage. The muscles in my face twitched as I tried to force the worry out of my expression, but he showed no indication that he noticed my unease.

Robin glanced between Sage and Emma. "Do you two ladies mind if I have a word alone with Crystal?"

Sage and Emma both nodded and walked off together to a nearby booth.

I looked up into Robin's eyes, my own beginning to glisten with tears. "Robin, you shouldn't be here."

His hands came up to rest on my biceps. "I couldn't stand not talking to you. Whatever it is, we can work this out. I needed to see you in person. Plus, I couldn't let my authentic peg leg go to waste."

I glanced down at his leg and almost laughed. He was right when he said I'd like his costume. When I looked back up into his eyes, though, my chest constricted, and my throat closed up. They shouldn't all be here at the same time.

"Robin," I said quietly, "I told you I didn't want you to come."

"I know, but I'm a stubborn guy. I want to talk about it, whatever it is."

"Robin, I—" I paused. It was going to happen one

way or another. The three people I loved most were here in one spot, and as much as I wanted to stop it, I knew now that I couldn't control the future. It was best to simply enjoy the present.

I swallowed the lump in my throat before speaking. "I'm glad you're here right now. Let's just have fun, okay?"

He pulled me into a hug and kissed the top of my head, which really ended up being a kiss on my pointed witch hat. "That sounds like a good idea. I love you, Crystal."

I had to force the tears back. "I love you, too, Robin."

He took my hand, which helped steady it, and led me over to Sage and Emma.

"So." Emma looked between us with bright eyes. "Where should we start?"

Robin looked around before gesturing to the carnival game in front of us. "This looks like as good of place as any."

We spent the next half hour making our way down the aisle. I tried to let go and have fun, but my senses — all but my sixth one — were on full alert. I jumped when a balloon popped and tensed when a nearby child screamed in excitement.

Robin gave my hand a gentle squeeze. "You okay?"

I gazed up at him and gave a fake shrug. "Yeah. I'm fine."

I'm not fine, I wanted to say. *But if it comes down to it,*

I hope you *will be.*

Emma hopped in excitement when her ring landed on the end of a bottle. Sage high-fived her in congratulations.

Emma turned toward me. "Let's head down the next aisle. I want to visit your mom's tent."

"No," I said too quickly. Everyone seemed to notice, and I quickly forced myself to relax. "I mean, it's a popular booth, so maybe we should wait until a little later in the night. Then there won't be a line." Hopefully my friends would forget about it or be too tired to visit her. I couldn't let the three people I loved most be together.

"Okay, well, we can at least go see how long the line is," Emma suggested.

"How about we go through the haunted forest," I countered. "There will be a longer line for it when it gets really dark out, so we shouldn't have to wait now."

"We already went down the haunted trail," Sage pointed out.

"Come on." Robin pulled at my hand. "Let's just go down the next aisle."

Emma rushed off in front of us, and I had no choice but to follow as Robin dragged me behind him.

"I guess you were right," Emma said, looking toward my mom's tent. "There is a long line."

I followed her gaze and noticed curly brown hair at the front of the line. I had the sudden urge to call out to him and get him to join our group before a sinking feeling in my chest reminded me that Emma and Derek didn't want to be by each other right now. If he wasn't hanging with us, who was he hanging out with? Hadn't he said he wasn't going to come?

I watched as my mother pulled aside the flap on her tent and a young girl stepped out. She rushed over to a man I guessed to be her dad and jumped in excitement. She was probably telling him about the fortune she'd received. Derek stepped into the tent behind my mom.

"I kind of want to try the apple bobbing booth," Sage admitted.

I pulled my gaze from my mother's tent and back to my friends. "You can go ahead. I don't really want to right now."

"Yeah," Emma agreed with me, "I'll mess up my makeup."

"I'll try apple bobbing with you," Robin offered, releasing my hand.

A moment later, a voice called my name from behind me. I turned to find Hope dressed as a unicorn rushing toward me with a smile on her face. She plowed into me and squeezed me into a tight hug.

I hugged her back. "Hey, Hope! Are you having fun?"

"Yes!" she answered enthusiastically. "Look what I won!" She held up a small stuffed animal shaped like a cat.

"That's awesome!" I answered just as Hope's mom, Melinda, caught up with her.

"Hi, Crystal," Melinda said, taking Hope's hand. "How was volleyball season?"

"It was good. I'm kind of sad it's over."

"Yeah, but at least you have another season. You'll be ready to start babysitting again on Monday, right?"

I couldn't look her in the eyes, so I stared down at the cat in Hope's hands instead. "I hope so," was all I could say.

"Well, have fun at the rest of the festival," Melinda told me with a wave while Hope dragged her off toward a new game.

I nodded back. "You, too."

I turned back toward my friends, who were giggling their heads off at the apple bobbing booth. Robin came up for air, still hopeless in the apple department. I couldn't help but laugh along when he plunged his head back under the water and fought with an apple that bounced away from him every time he came close. Sage pulled her head out of the water, and her hands shot up in victory. An apple was trapped between her teeth, and Robin was still engaged in a losing battle. Mine and Emma's laughter only grew louder, but a split second later when I heard my mother's voice, my laughter died. I turned toward the sound, facing the stage. A woman dressed as a gypsy stood at the microphone and was trying to get everyone's attention. It was the first time the microphone had been turned on all night since the band wasn't scheduled to start playing for another half hour.

Emma noticed me staring. "Crystal, what's your mom doing?"

"Can I please have everyone's attention?" she repeated into the microphone.

"I don't know," I answered Emma. "Maybe Sheryl and Tammy asked her to make an announcement." I inched my way down the aisle until I stood at the back of the grassy area in front of the stage.

Conversations seemed to die out around us, and the area grew quiet. When my mother was satisfied that she had enough of the audience's attention, she spoke again.

"I'm sorry to interrupt your night, but I have an announcement to make, and it can't wait." She glanced toward the side of the stage and then back at the audience. "It's not so much an announcement as a confession, and it's time that I spoke up."

A confession? What could she be talking about?

"Crystal," Emma repeated from beside me, "what's your mom doing?"

The hairs on my arms stood up, and I couldn't answer. More people had gathered around the stage to listen.

My mother continued. "I think it's time that Peyton Springs knew the truth." She hesitated and glanced off stage. For a moment, an eerie silence hung in the air before she spoke again. "My tarot card booth you all like, the one you all say is so accurate . . . well, it's for real."

My heart nearly stopped in my chest. She told me

she'd never tell the community. Why was she doing this now?

She didn't stop. "The truth is, I'm not who you all think I am. Because of what I can do, I've hurt people, and it's time you all know the story of Sam Marshall."

21

I didn't give myself another second to ask questions. Something was seriously wrong. I didn't know what it was yet, but I knew I had to stop my mother from telling the whole town our secret. Even she said it was best if the town didn't know. I pushed through the crowd as she began her story. When I rushed up the stairs on the side of the stage, I immediately noticed a figure standing with his back toward me. His arms were crossed over his chest, and he was staring at my mom on stage.

I drew in a deep breath. "Derek, do you have any idea what's going on? Why is my mom doing this?"

He turned to me slowly, a wide smile plastered on his face.

My pulse quickened. "Derek, what's going on?"

If possible, I could swear his grin grew wider. He spoke as if amused. "You're so stupid."

I took a step back, stunned. "Derek, what's *wrong* with you? You've never been as mean as you have lately. You haven't been acting like yourself . . ."

He noticed the realization cross my face, and he nodded in satisfaction.

I distanced myself another step until I gripped the railing to the stairs. My eyes widened in horror, and I completely froze in place. How could I not have realized it before? Derek had been so different lately. I had assumed something major was bothering him, but nothing made enough sense to cause such a drastic change. I should have paid closer attention, done my research, and realized such a thing was possible.

I spoke slowly. "You're not Derek, are you? You haven't been for a long time."

"Bingo." He laughed.

"Oh, my god!" I cried. Worry about my mother's confession faded as I faced the new problem standing right in front of me. "Who are you? What have you done to Derek?"

"Oh, relax," he said like we were having the most casual conversation in the world. "He's still in here." He tapped his head with his index finger. "I just needed to borrow him for a while."

"A while? How long has it been?" I quickly shifted through my memory, trying to remember when Derek had changed. It was around the time I had stayed home from school, when we held that séance. A gasp escaped my lips, and my hand flew to my mouth in shock. I knew now why I hadn't seen the shadow ghost since we held the séance. The ghost was never my father to begin with.

"You possessed him when we contacted you," I accused. That's what the explosion of energy was about. Anger boiled in my blood, momentarily masking my fear.

He began pacing, but at least he was keeping a generous amount of distance between us. It was strange to watch Derek move in front of me, knowing it wasn't him who was speaking. "Hmm . . . maybe you're not as stupid as I thought."

Suddenly, a lot more about the past few weeks made sense. "Derek never broke up with Emma, did he? It was *you*."

"Ah, so maybe you are a bright girl."

"My headaches? That was you, too?" My heart hammered against my rib cage, and I thought I might nearly fall over. Luckily, I was still gripping onto the railing to steady myself.

"I was wondering when you'd catch on to that one. I mean, come on," he spread his arms wide mockingly, "you only got headaches when I was around."

And my headache was only returning again. I wanted to put as much distance as I could between myself and the man standing in front of me, but if Derek really was still in there somewhere, I couldn't just abandon him.

"How did you know so much about Derek?" I asked in an attempt to make sense of it all. I forced my breath to slow. I couldn't let him see how much he was terrifying me.

He shrugged. "I didn't. I just played along. It was so simple. I claimed I lost his locker combination, and the school gave me his class schedule. When I didn't know how to get to the kid's house, I asked your friend to walk me home a couple of times. I mostly didn't talk to the kid's family. And you were easy to convince. It's like you didn't even know enough about your friend to tell the difference."

"I did!" I defended. I knew *something* was up, but never in a million years would I have guessed it was a *possession*. I didn't even know for sure that was possible, not until now. I briefly thought back to the time Olivia Owen spoke through me. She'd done the same thing to Kelli. But I'd never thought of it as possession. She hadn't actually inhabited my body; she'd just spoken through me. Was this the same type of thing?

He stopped pacing and stood still in front of me, tapping his foot. "There's so much you still don't know, Crystal."

I swallowed, forcing my voice to remain strong. "Who are you?"

His brows shot up. "You haven't figured that one out yet?" He glanced behind himself at my mother, who was still giving her confession at the microphone.

I knew I had to get to her, but I couldn't with him in my way. I wasn't even sure which was more important at the moment: my mom or Derek?

He scoffed. "Figures she never mentioned me." His hard gaze met mine, sending my heart pounding again. He plastered a smile of amusement back on his face. "You see, Crystal, I'm the guy your mother killed."

I drew in a sharp, hot breath. "You have the wrong person. My mother never killed anyone." My grip tightened around the railing.

He threw back his head and laughed. It was the kind of laugh that sent a shiver down my spine. He began pacing again. "The wrong person? I don't think so. Not this time."

I forced myself to speak evenly even though my breathing wavered. "This time?"

"When I first saw you on the SMU campus, I thought *you* were your mother. You have the same blond hair, same blue eyes, and same nose. You see, at first, I didn't realize how much time had passed. I saw this girl around campus that I could have sworn was Theresa, and all of a sudden, it's like I woke up. The strange thing was, I still knew what had happened to me. Then you showed up, and I followed you. It wasn't until I actually saw your mother that I realized you weren't her. And then the rest made sense. They called you Crystal Frost, so I knew that meant Andrea had married David. I didn't know who the new guy was, though. Teddy? That's his name, right? So, tell me. What happened to David, then?"

The surprise on my face as he spoke was evident in my wide eyes. Could he really mean Theresa Hanson, Justine's mom? And if he knew my parents, that meant . . .

"You're Sam Marshall," I stated confidently. It wasn't a question.

He missed a step in his pace and then planted his feet firmly on the ground. "So, you *have* heard of me. Interesting . . ."

It all made sense now. Justine had said she felt like someone was watching her, and she was right. It was Sam all along. He thought Justine was her mother, and somehow that awakened his spirit. Then he'd been following her around campus.

"That's why you went into the shop asking my mom about college. You wanted to make sure she was the right person. Derek never was worried about his future."

He nodded with a haunting grin that made my skin crawl. "Right again."

"You were so interested in her, always asking to come over to my house or go to the shop. And Diane's visions? She said it was like she was seeing her own memories through someone else's eyes. She was talking about the day you died. She was seeing it from *your* perspective." Everything that happened over the last few weeks finally came together in my mind. I didn't need my sixth sense to confirm it.

"Well, I don't know anything about what things those *witches* see," Sam responded.

I had the sudden urge to punch him in the face at the term, but I still saw Derek standing in front of me and couldn't bring myself to hurt him. Derek wasn't exactly a huge guy, but I wasn't big either. I'd have a hard time fighting him.

"I see you've joined them," he said, gesturing to my costume.

I gritted my teeth but only reacted by raising my voice. "So, what is this?" I gestured to my mom on stage, who still hadn't noticed me. She was nearing the end of Sam's story. I caught a glimpse of Sophie and Diane near the stairs on the other end of the stage. They were watching my mom as warily as I was, no doubt wondering whether they should stop her or not.

Sam laughed again, and though he was in Derek's body, it didn't sound anything like my friend. "It's my revenge, of course. You were actually the one to give me the idea."

I released the clench on my jaw to speak. "How do you figure that?"

"At first, I thought I'd just kill her. An eye for an eye. I even tried a couple of times."

My breath quickened, and another piece of the puzzle came together. That's why my mom had been so clumsy lately. "The box cutter that could have slit her wrist, the crystal ball that could have cracked her skull, her tripping on the rug . . . That was all *you*!"

His laughter never seemed to end. "Of course it was!"

"You were there each time," I thought aloud. "First as a ghost, then in Derek's body."

"Right again. I even tried killing you when I thought you were your mother."

I instantly thought back to the bus ride back from SMU and the tree that would have fallen on our bus had I not screamed. Did that mean he had something to do with my first accident? *No*, I thought almost immediately. That happened before I visited SMU. All this stuff with Sam happened only after we spotted each other in the cafeteria that day.

"I was beginning to lose my patience," he continued. "After all, it took some extra energy to make the objects move seemingly on their own. I had to wait a bit for my energy to return and try again. I could have framed the kid," he gestured to Derek's body with a shrug, "but he didn't have anything to do with it. I just needed a body for the time being so I could actually communicate with people. It's not like you were any help with that."

I almost bit back with an explanation about why I hadn't been able to help him earlier, but he continued without missing a beat.

"Then you mentioned a better revenge is public humiliation. And you were *so* right. Now she has to *live* with what she's done!"

"Sam," I pleaded. "I can help you. She didn't kill

you. It wasn't her fault. Can't we talk this out?"

He threw his head back to laugh again. It made me sick to see the satisfaction he was getting out of this.

"You can't help me," he snarled. "You can't *change* this. Besides, the secret is already out. Your mom is almost done with her confession."

"Why is she doing this?"

He shrugged. "Because I told her that if she didn't confess to killing me, I'd kill you instead."

I wanted to run, to get as far away from him as I could so he wouldn't hurt me, but my feet remained grounded. I surprised myself when I managed to spit my next words out instead of cowering away like instinct told me to do. "Why are you telling me all this?"

"I've been dying to tell *someone*," he answered hauntingly. "And it's fun watching you try to figure it all out."

Sam glanced to my mom on stage. She was reaching her closing remarks, and we both fell silent to listen.

"I cannot take back what I did," she said, "and I can't change who I am, a wi—" She paused like the word was too hard to spit out. "A witch," she finished.

I glared at Sam, though he didn't notice. He'd made her say that; I didn't need my sixth sense to know she wouldn't use that word on her own.

The entire bandstand area went quiet for several long seconds until someone in the crowd clapped their hands and shouted. "Great story, Andrea."

Sam and I shifted to stare out at what we could see

of the crowd. They weren't taking her seriously.

Sam balled Derek's hands into fists. "This was supposed to work!" He spoke as if I wasn't there.

My mother's voice filled the stage area again. "I am completely serious. This thing I can do, it's why Divination is part of our town."

An unfamiliar voice called from the crowd. "Props for being true to yourself!"

In that moment, it was clear. Half of our town didn't even believe her, and the other half accepted her for who she was.

I relaxed slightly and spoke to Sam confidently. "It appears you won't get your revenge."

He scoffed and turned to me. "You know what the cool thing about possession is?" He didn't wait for an answer. "Even though I'm in someone else's body, I still have some power."

I remembered what my mom had said about how ghosts were more powerful the longer they'd been dead. That must have been how he could possess Derek.

"It's not as much as when I'm outside the body," he continued. "You see, it takes a lot of energy to keep control of this body. After I try something . . . powerful, I have to rest, but since I haven't tried anything in a couple of days, I have just enough energy . . ." He paused as if mocking me, and then his eyes shifted to the stage lights hanging above my mother.

My gaze followed his, and in a split second, my world seemed to crash down around me. My heart slammed against my chest, and I could hardly breathe. One of the stage lights swung from its safety cable.

I didn't even think about what I was doing when I pushed past Sam and sprinted across the stage. I shoved my mother from where she stood in front of the microphone the moment the safety cable snapped.

22

Realizing I'd narrowly escaped Sam's attack, I whirled toward him a second later and raced across the stage, tackling Derek's body to the ground. I pulled my fist back and momentarily caught the fear that crossed his expression. It didn't slow me down. Though it was Derek's face, I could see Sam in his eyes. My fist came down, slamming into his solid cheekbone. I pulled back again, this time aiming for his nose. Before I could land another punch, a set of hands gripped my shoulders to pull me off of Sam.

"Stop!" I screamed to whoever was behind me. I struggled away, trying once again to somehow make Sam feel pain, to get back at him for trying to hurt my mom. "He tried to kill her!" I screamed.

"Crystal, calm down," a male voice said into my

ear. He gripped onto my shoulders so tightly that there was no use trying to fight my way out of his grasp. I was still too full of fury to place the voice behind me.

"Please!" I cried, finally giving up the struggle. I slowly turned to face the man who had pulled me off of Sam, and when I met his eyes, my knees went weak. I couldn't move or speak, only stare into the eyes of my father. How was this possible? He looked the same as I remembered him from my childhood and from pictures I'd saved of him. A bright glow from one of the stage lights behind him outlined his silhouette.

"Crystal," he said again.

"I—I don't understand." I looked up at him, my eyes watering and my body completely still. "How are you here?" I forced my gaze down to his hands, which were still on me, and moved my own hands to touch his. He was so solid, so real. I spoke slowly when I looked up into his eyes again. "I don't get it. How did you come back? How is this possible?"

He swallowed hard. "I'm not back. Crystal, it's you . . ."

He turned, and I stared past him to where he was looking. This time, I fell to my knees. My father let go of me, and my hands came to my mouth. In front of me lay my body, sprawled out next to the stage light that had crashed on top of me. My mother, Sophie, and Diane knelt next to my unmoving form.

After the initial wave of shock hit me, I was able to look back up at my father. That bright glow behind him remained.

"I'm dead?" I asked in a small voice.

He nodded somberly.

It's easier to accept death when you know there's an afterlife, but this was just unreal. I hadn't felt any pain, and I certainly felt *alive*.

"Don't move," my father said sternly.

My gaze jerked in the direction he was looking, and I noticed he was talking to Sam, who was slowly creeping toward the stairs. He stopped as soon as my father's voice boomed in his direction. Sam cowered but didn't move.

I glanced between Sam and my father. "How did I—?"

I didn't have to finish my sentence. My father understood what I meant. How was I, as a ghost, able to interact with Derek's body as if I were still solid myself?

"Sam still has one foot on this plane, so you can interact with him. Since he's still in your friend's body, those interactions will affect both the spirit inside and the body he's controlling."

"And you?" I asked. "I don't understand. I thought you'd crossed over."

My father smiled like the answer was so simple. "I did. Remember the folklore about the veil between the living and the dead being open on Halloween? Well, it's true. Plus, I haven't gone very far."

He glanced behind him, and for the first time, I noticed five other figures on stage with him. The stage lights glowed behind them, giving off the same effect they had when I first turned to my father moments before. The lights were so bright that I could hardly make out the figures' faces. My father shifted, and the light followed. That's when it clicked. It wasn't the stage lights at all. It was the light to the other side. Each spirit on stage had their own, as if each was a doorway they'd stepped through to visit me tonight. I looked back at the other five figures, and one by one, I noticed they all looked familiar. Tears welled in my eyes.

"We've all been watching over you," my father admitted.

I rose from the ground and stepped toward them, completely in shock. My eyes locked first on the tall teenage girl with blond hair and brown eyes. "Olivia?"

She nodded, and I fell into her in an embrace. Olivia was the first ghost I saw a year ago when my abilities manifested.

"Whoa, Crystal," she laughed.

I pulled away, staring into her eyes. I couldn't help but crack a nervous smile that almost made the tears go away. I sniffled. "How has life been on the other side?"

She smiled back. "It's wonderful." She'd always looked like an angel, but with the bright glow behind her, I now believed that she was. "I've kept my promises," she told me. "I've been watching over Kelli this whole time."

I blinked away the last of the remaining tears. "She's changed, and it's all been for the better, thanks to you." My eyes drifted to the faces of the next two figures. A young girl with green eyes and dark hair held onto an older man's hand. "Penny. Scott."

"We saw you," Penny told me. "We've been watching Hope and my mom this past year, and we saw you visiting Hope."

"I did. I was her babysitter. How's your mom, by the way?"

"She's doing much better," Scott answered. "Lauren is getting the help she needed."

"That's great to hear."

The other girl with them inched forward, and I recognized her, too. I'd only seen her once, but she helped me save Sage's life.

"Melissa." I greeted her like I was reconnecting with an old friend, even though we'd only ever spoken a few words to each other.

"Hi, Crystal. I never got a chance to thank you. You know, for saving my sister's life."

"Don't worry about it. I see you crossed over."

A smile stretched across her face. "I did a long time ago. I was already crossed over when I met you. It took a lot of energy to get to you, but it helped to have my sister nearby. She always gave me strength."

That explained why she'd been so transparent when most of the ghosts I saw appeared solid and why I only saw her the one time. She didn't have enough energy to come to me in full form.

Finally, I focused on the fifth figure standing next

to Melissa. The girl looked a little older than me, right about at the prime of her life.

"I'm sorry, but I don't remember you," I admitted sheepishly. "Did I ever help you in some way?"

An amused expression crossed her face. "It has been a while, hasn't it? I've certainly changed." She glanced down at herself. "Don't you remember me, Crystal? We used to be best friends."

I didn't understand and immediately shifted through my memory, wondering if there was a girl I'd forgotten. It didn't make any sense since Emma had always been my best friend ever since Kindergarten. I was about to ask her name when it suddenly clicked. She was the best friend I had *before* Emma, my first ghost, my imaginary friend.

"Eva!"

She nodded.

"But you were so young. Shouldn't you look like you did?"

She giggled in amusement. "We don't always stay the way we die. The young grow older, and the old grow younger on the other side. For a while, we keep the identities we had when we died, but eventually, you realize that age doesn't really matter on the other side."

"That's . . . actually kind of amazing." I glanced back toward my father. "Is it time for me to go? What are you all doing here? Are you here to guide me into the light?"

He shook his head. "We're here to watch over you,

Crystal. First, we have a few things to take care of, starting with Sam."

Sam hadn't moved from his position on the floor where my father had told him to stop. I wasn't sure if he was scared of my father himself or of the many spirits around him. Like my father had said, Sam was still partially on the spiritual plane, and all the other spirits around him could now interact with him. He was no longer the most powerful one around.

"Sam," my father said, kneeling down to his level. "It's time for you to let go."

The evil laugh Sam was so good at returned. "I'm not going anywhere until Andrea pays for what she did to me."

"Come on, Sam," my father tried to reason. "We were good friends. You have to trust me that Andrea would never purposely hurt *anyone*."

"We were friends a long time ago," Sam spat, still not moving from his position on the ground.

I stood behind my father, wondering if there was some way I could help, but he seemed to have the situation under control.

My father shook his head in response to Sam. "It doesn't seem that long ago to you, though, does it? You only recently awakened. That's why you're still so angry. To you, your death just happened, but it's been years, Sam. Your family has found peace. *Theresa* has found peace. Come with me into the light. You'll find peace there."

"There's nothing for me there! Everything I loved is *here*, and Andrea took that away from me."

"You're remembering it wrong," my father insisted. "Andrea was trying to save your life. Why can't you see that?"

As my father and Sam talked, my gaze drifted toward my body on stage. Emma and Robin now knelt next to me. Teddy leaned over my body and administered some sort of makeshift first aid. I couldn't really see it since there were so many people crowded around the scene. My mother had dropped to her knees just feet away, and Sophie and Diane were attempting to console her. Beyond that, a crowd of onlookers observed from the grass at the front of the stage. I recognized each and every one of them.

First, I saw Hope and her mom, who both had tears in their eyes. Emma's mom and her little sister, Kate, stood next to them. Kate raised herself on her toes, trying to get a good look. Beside them was Derek's family, including his mom, dad, and twin sisters. Sage was also nearby, her eyes filling with tears. Finally, I spotted Kelli and Justine.

They were all here, everyone I loved, everyone I'd ever helped.

A police officer was trying to push people back, telling them to give me some space. *It's no use*, I thought. *I'm already gone*. It had only been minutes since it all happened, but the ambulance that was nearly here wasn't going to be any help, not now.

Movement caught my eye, and I noticed one more person I recognized in the crowd, Justine's mother, Theresa. She pulled Justine into a comforting hug.

"Sam," I blurted, interrupting my father. "Look!" I pointed to Theresa, and his gaze followed. "Look at Theresa. She has a daughter now. She has a family."

Justine looked up into Theresa's eyes before resting her head on her mother's shoulder.

"Look at their family. Theresa has moved on, and she's found happiness." I turned to face him fully and then knelt beside him like my father was doing. "My mother didn't hurt you. She was trying to save you. You were hurt because you didn't have faith in her. If you can't have faith in my mother, think about Theresa. One day, she's going to make it to the other side. She's going to expect you to be waiting there for her, but what is she going to find if you're still seeking revenge? What will she think of you if you manage to kill one of her friends? You're better than this, Sam."

He didn't say a thing. He simply stared out into the crowd, his eyes locked on Theresa. I noticed the way they softened and brightened when he spotted her, like she was all that mattered to him. And that's when I realized the truth.

"It's not about my mother and her prediction, is it?" I asked quietly. "It never was. You weren't mad that she warned you about your death. You were angry that you never got to live the life you dreamed of with Theresa, and you needed someone to blame, someone to take your anger out on. Sam, you can be with Theresa again, but you have to find peace and go into the light."

Sam finally tore his gaze from Theresa and looked me in the eyes. "I had so much planned for us. We were supposed to grow old together." His voice was so small that he almost didn't seem like the Sam I'd just been talking to.

"It won't seem like any time at all before she joins you on the other side," my father promised. He turned to me and rested a hand on my shoulder. "It seems like Crystal was only a child a week ago, and now she's a beautiful young woman." He looked back at Sam. "Your life with Theresa isn't the only one you get to live. Someday, she'll be with you again in another life."

Sam blinked a few times and then stared across the stage. I glanced back to see what he was looking at, but I didn't spot anything.

"That's your light," my father said.

Sam's voice grew soft. "That's—that's my dad. I didn't know . . ."

My father looked back toward the light I couldn't see. "He's been waiting a long time for you."

Sam swallowed hard. "You're sure Theresa will join me one day? I mean, she lived a whole lifetime without me. Will she even remember me?"

My father nodded. "You have nothing to be afraid of."

"I don't want to go," Sam pleaded. "I just found her again. She's right in front of me, yet so far out of reach."

"And you will find her once more," my father promised in a calm voice. "Be there for her at the light like your father is for you now."

Sam's eyes shifted between the light I couldn't see and Theresa, but they eventually stayed on the light. He visibly reacted as if his dad was speaking to him.

"It's time," my father said.

Sam took a deep breath. "Okay. I'll do it for Theresa. I'll be there waiting for her."

I couldn't believe what I was seeing next. It was like my eyes were playing tricks on me. One second I was seeing Derek's face, and then next, an unfamiliar image washed over it until I was only seeing Sam. His outline was so familiar, but his face was new to me. Derek's body dropped to the ground, and Sam's spirit stood.

He turned back briefly before fading away. "Hey. Tell your mother I'm sorry." And then he took two more steps before he was gone.

I quickly looked back at Derek. "Is he okay?" I asked my father, frantically searching for signs of life.

"He will be," my father promised, "but right now, we don't have much time."

"Is it time for me to cross over? Why didn't I see Sam's light and you did? Is it because I haven't crossed over yet? But I can see your light. Where's my light?" The questions tumbled out of me.

My father answered quickly like he was pressed for time. "You're correct. You couldn't see Sam's light because you haven't crossed over. You can see mine because it's a different type of doorway, if you will. You don't have one because you're not ready to go yet."

"What do you mean I'm not ready to go yet? I don't have any unfinished business. I already said goodbye to everyone. I did what you told me to do. I saved . . ." My voice trailed off. Why he had told me to save three people when I only needed to save my mom? Did his warning somehow change the future? How were Robin and Emma involved?

Oh. Now I knew exactly what he had meant. It never was about Robin and Emma.

"It doesn't matter right now." He stood and grabbed my hand to pull me up, leading me over to the center of the stage.

By now, there was an ambulance crew surrounding my body.

"Clear," one of the EMTs shouted before shocking my body with an AED.

I looked back toward my father. "It's no use. I'm already dead."

"That AED might not save you, but we can." He glanced toward the five other spirits on stage. "There's so much love surrounding you tonight, Crystal. It may just be enough to revive you."

My brow furrowed. "What do you mean?"

He only answered with a smile.

The six spirits on stage stepped closer to my body. They didn't even regard the EMTs next to me. My father, Olivia, Penny, Scott, Melissa, and Eva all gathered around to place their hands on my heart. I couldn't help it when I began sobbing happy tears in response. My father gestured for me to join them. I knelt down beside my own body, closed my eyes, and took a deep breath for courage. Then I placed my hand on top of all of theirs.

"Clear," the EMT shouted again.

I opened my eyes and stared down at my unmoving form. My eyes widened in shock at what I saw. A pale white glow emanated from each spirit's hand, all but mine. I watched in amazement as light originated somewhere near their hearts and traveled down their arms to end at their hands. Another pulse of light journeyed from their hearts to mine. Each time the light reached their hands, the brightness grew until it was almost blinding. I witnessed that light fill my body, bringing color back to my cheeks.

"I'm going to miss you all," I managed to say through the tears before the EMT shouted one last time and shocked my heart back to life.

23

I awoke to a white room, where the sun spilled into every corner. Sorrow flowed through me, igniting my senses as if they weren't my own. I forced my body to awaken further until I realized there were hands holding mine. In the next second, I sprang up in the bed I was lying in, fully alert. The sorrow I was feeling *wasn't* my own. It was my mother's and Robin's, the two people who were hanging onto me.

I was back.

I wasn't just alive. The light my father and the other spirits filled me with had blessed me in ways I didn't think possible. My abilities had returned at full force.

But it wasn't just that. My full range of senses seemed heightened. It was like the last few weeks with my faded abilities had caused my other senses to deteriorate with them, and now that my gift was back, so was everything else. I could smell the daisies in the corner of the hospital room, and the blond of my mother's hair appeared brighter than it had yesterday — at least, I thought it was only yesterday.

"How long have I been out?" I asked before either of them could say anything.

A look a relief crossed Robin's face. "Over 15 hours."

My mother gave my right hand a squeeze. "Crystal, I'm so glad you're okay."

A grin formed across my face. After everything that happened, that statement couldn't be any truer. I really *was* okay, better than I'd ever felt, to be honest.

"Don't worry about me, Mom. I'm glad *you're* okay."

"Derek told us everything," Robin said quickly. "He told us about Sam, about the possession."

I breathed a sigh of relief. "Derek's okay?"

My mother nodded. "They took him to the hospital, too, but he's okay now. He told them he passed out because he was queasy from seeing what happened to you."

The thing was, I could actually see Derek doing that had he not been possessed.

"He told us what he remembered while you were asleep," my mother informed me.

I blinked a few times, absorbing this information. "So, he remembers being possessed?"

My mother looked toward the door. "Why don't you ask him?"

I followed her gaze, and my body relaxed as Emma and Derek walked into the room hand in hand. "Derek! Are you okay?"

His brows shot up. "Me? What about you?"

"I'm fine. What do you remember?"

Derek and Emma stopped at the foot of the bed. "I came in and out. Some if it I remember, some of it I don't. It was like I was there the whole time, but I couldn't control my own body. I wanted to give you guys some sort of sign, but I couldn't break through."

"I should have known it wasn't him," Emma admitted. "The real Derek would've never broken up with me."

Derek's expression softened as he stared into Emma's eyes. "No, I wouldn't."

Emma couldn't hold it in any longer. She flung her arms around Derek's neck and held onto him so tightly that his face began turning red.

He pulled away with a laugh. "Don't worry about me. I'm okay. None of us have ever gone through something like this. I didn't even know it was *possible* to be possessed. If it had happened to any of you, I wouldn't have guessed what was really going on, either. I'm just glad Sam's gone and I have control of my body again."

"I'm glad, too," I told him. "I feel so terrible for not seeing the signs. It's just, the possibility never crossed my mind. I thought something else was bothering you."

"Believe me, if something was wrong, I'd talk to you about it," he assured me.

The door to the hospital room clicked open again, and Teddy slipped inside. He looked from me to my mother, then back at me. "You're awake."

I nodded. "I'm fine, really."

He leaned out of the room for a moment, and a second later, Sophie and Diane entered behind him. Teddy shoved his hands into the pockets of his jeans and came to stand at my bedside. Now my whole family was here.

I turned to Robin. "I'm so sorry about everything that's happened between us recently. I just . . ." I honestly didn't know what to say.

"You knew," Robin accused lightly, stopping me.

I tilted my head at him, wondering what he meant.

"You knew something bad was going to happen," he clarified. "That's why you didn't want me to come to the festival."

"I figured the same thing," Emma admitted. "You were trying to convince me not to come, either."

I could hardly believe how well they knew me, but it also brought me comfort. There was no point in lying to them any longer. "I'm sorry. I knew that if you all knew something was going to happen, you'd want to try to save me, and I had to save you." My gaze drifted toward my mother as I spoke.

"But why me and Robin?" Emma asked. "If it was

about your mom, why keep us two away?"

I swallowed hard, not taking my eyes off my mom. Her expression was soft, but tears were beginning to well in her eyes.

"I didn't know what exactly was supposed to happen," I told them, still looking at her. "I was just covering my bases, trying to keep you all safe. I was told I had to save three of the people I love most." That was the way my father worded it. Three *of* the people I loved most. Not *the* three people I loved most like I had been assuming all along. "In reality, Emma and Robin were never in any real danger. It was my mom and my siblings."

My mother's expression quickly shifted to one of surprise. "Siblings?"

I nodded. "I know you didn't want to know, but I can't hold it in any longer. Mom, we were both right. You're having twins, a boy and a girl."

Emma squealed. "Congratulations!"

Teddy froze, and a stunned expression fell across his face. Even as Sophie and Diane patted him on the back in congratulations, he didn't move. Only after my mother made her way around the bed and pulled him into a hug was he able to speak. "We—we're going to have twins? We're going to have twins!" He hugged my mother again.

As everyone else was congratulating them, Robin took a moment to lean over me to whisper in my ear. "Crystal Frost, what you did for your mother was incredibly brave. You never cease to amaze me."

I shrugged my shoulders up slowly. I didn't know what else to say. He was so close to me now that his lips hovered just inches above my own, taking my breath away.

His eyes shifted over my face, and then he whispered the words that let me know everything was finally okay with us again. "I am in love with you." And then his lips connected with mine. Far too soon, he pulled away to sit back down in his chair.

My mother came back around her side of the bed and wrapped her arms around me. Her voice cracked when she spoke. "I'm so proud of you, Crystal. I couldn't have done it without you."

I pulled away, a perplexed expression written on my face. "You couldn't have done what without me?"

She blinked away tears. "Admitted my secret to everyone. It was something you said just before the festival. You said your witch costume was about telling the world it didn't matter what they thought about you, that you loved yourself for who you were. It just hit me that I'd been hiding behind the idea of make-believe for too long. I wondered what I'd been doing all these years trying to hide it when you've only had your abilities for a year and already embraced them fully. I found my courage through you, Crystal."

It wasn't until she said it that it dawned on me how comfortable and confident I actually was with my abilities. And with my mom's secret out in the open, I didn't have to hide it for her sake anymore, either.

The room fell silent for a beat until Sophie spoke. "We're so glad you're okay, Crystal."

I sat up straighter in my hospital bed. "I'm better than okay."

With all eyes on me, I noticed how incredibly lucky I was to have so many people who cared about me. They had all helped guide me through every challenge I'd been through over the last year. I thought back to the day I'd visited Sage, about how I realized she'd found her calling through music and I thought I'd found mine by having to die for the people I loved. But there were people out there who believed I was destined for better things, and I was determined to fulfill that destiny. From here on out, I was no longer just Crystal Frost. I was Crystal Frost, Psychic.

ABOUT THE AUTHOR

Alicia Rades is a USA Today bestselling author of young adult paranormal fiction with a love for supernatural stories set in the modern world. When she's not plotting out fiction novels, you can find her writing content for various websites or plowing her way through her never-ending reading list. Alicia holds a bachelor's degree in communications with an emphasis on professional writing.

Made in the USA
Middletown, DE
24 April 2018